BT

228

CROOKED FOOT'S GOLD

Jim and Barney are trailing a thief when they arrive at White Rock, but they become drawn into the mysterious community that is claimed by white gold-seekers and restless tribes alike. Then, a dying renegade tells them the story of Crooked Foot's gold, which leads to their being hunted down themselves, without knowing why. Now they must venture into dangerous territory seeking answers . . . and who knows what perils await them?

Books by Greg Mitchell
in the Linford Western Library:

OUTLAW VENGEANCE
RED ROCK CROSSING
KILLER'S KINGDOM
THE RAIDERS
MURDERING WELLS

GREG MITCHELL

◆

CROOKED FOOT'S GOLD

Complete and Unabridged

LINFORD
Leicester

First published in Great Britain in 2011 by
Robert Hale Limited, London

First Linford Edition
published 2012
by arrangement with
Robert Hale Limited, London

British Library CIP Data

Mitchell, Greg, *1935 –*
    Crooked Foot's gold.- -
    (Linford western library)
    1. Western stories.
    2. Large type books.
    I. Title II. Series
    823.9'14–dc23

    ISBN 978–1–4448–1204–6

Published by
F. A. Thorpe (Publishing)
Anstey, Leicestershire

Set by Words & Graphics Ltd.
Anstey, Leicestershire
Printed and bound in Great Britain by
T. J. International Ltd., Padstow, Cornwall

This book is printed on acid-free paper

1

Herb Andrews peered through the lens of his theodolite at the figure on the distant hill and waved a hand to indicate that the man holding the marker should move back a little. But the red-haired man did not seem to be watching for the surveyor's signals. He had twisted sideways and was looking to his right with a startled expression on his face.

Andrews was about to shout a reprimand for his inattention when the man crumpled. Almost simultaneously the sharp report of a gunshot reached him. The surveyor had never heard a Sioux war cry but he had no doubts about the spine-chilling sound from the nearby pine thicket. For a fraction of a second he remained frozen in disbelief, then turned and ran for the camp — he had a rifle there. Middle-aged and heavily built, Andrews had little chance of escaping but to remain where he was meant certain death.

At the sound of the shot, Joe Gilbert, the chainman, threw down the linked wire chain he was unpacking and drew a six-shooter. He had not been as trusting as his boss. Gilbert had spent years on the frontier and was loath to work unarmed so close to the Sioux reservation in country where hostile bands still roamed and so-called 'peaceful' tribesmen were allowed to travel and hunt.

'Run!' he shouted to his boss, as he stood his ground and looked for his first target. Already he was lining his sights on the mounted warriors breaking from the pines. They were still out of pistol range but would be there in a couple of seconds. He saw at a glance that there were too many to stop and could only hope that a few shots might discourage them. The hope was a slim one though, because he knew that he would be virtually defenceless when he fired the six shots in the gun; there was nowhere to run or even to take shelter while he reloaded. It was still long range for a revolver when he let go the first shot. As far as the shooter could see, it had little effect.

Andrews ran unsteadily toward the camp with a score of feather-decked, painted warriors urging their wiry ponies after him. The ponies covered a hundred yards of the uneven ground while the fleeing man was covering thirty. He was still too far from help when the leading warrior fired one shot at point-blank range and the surveyor was knocked face down to the ground. The warrior who had shot him, yelled in triumph and jumped from his pony to claim the scalp.

Another defensive shot came from Ned Black, the middle-aged camp cook who discharged a shotgun at the oncoming riders as he ran to join Gilbert. The range was hopelessly long and the weapon was loaded with light bird shot. If he had hoped to stay the rush, the plan did not succeed. A stray pellet or two might have stung a horse or rider but it did not deter them.

Gilbert fired wildly into the Sioux with no apparent effect and then, when his gun clicked empty, he turned and ran toward where the cook waited. Black had one shot left. His shotgun muzzle moved from target to target as he sought to do the most damage with his final cartridge.

Suddenly a spotted pony was at Gilbert's shoulder and a blow from a stone-headed war club smashed the chainman to the ground. But the warrior had no time to enjoy his easy victory. The cook fired and a close-range charge of shot sent the man somersaulting over his pony's tail.

His gun empty, Black reversed it and with the courage of one whose life was already forfeit, he flailed at the nearest rider with the butt. The attacker's pony jumped sideways and a brave following immediately behind, fired a flint-headed arrow into the white man's chest. Black was dying on his feet and probably did not notice when another warrior rode up and struck him with a coup stick. His knees buckled and, as he fell, a Sioux brave was already vaulting from his horse wielding a scalping knife.

A hundred yards from the camp, Henry Rhodes, wide-eyed in terror, squeezed his adolescent body down under the bank of a stream. He had been sent to get water for the cook and was not in full view of the attackers. For almost too long he watched his companions being cut down. Then self-preservation took over. Unarmed and terrified, he hid behind the low bank fearing to raise his head again in case he was seen. At any moment he expected to hear the tread of a Sioux pony or a shout of triumph when his hiding place was discovered. Surely they had seen him and would soon drag him away to be tortured to death.

For an hour he lay there shivering with cold and fear and listening to the warriors talking and laughing to each other while they looted the camp. He was all too aware that if some brave realized that the camp contained the belongings of five men and found only four bodies, the attackers would search about. But fortunately none did.

It seemed ages before he heard the warriors leave and even then Henry feared to raise his head above the level of the bank. What if some Indians were still in the camp? They could even be playing a cruel game with him. All sorts of horrifying situations were easy to imagine. Darkness had fallen when, cold and terrified, the boy climbed to his feet and looked around. Even in the poor light he could see that the Indians had taken all the survey party's mules. There might have been something he could have salvaged from the camp but terror had taken over. He feared what he knew he would find there. It was cold too when the sun had gone down and he briefly considered searching for a coat but in his shock and fear the boy decided against such a move. Instead he turned his face to the south and started walking. The mining settlement of White Rock was thirty miles away. He was not sure that he would reach it but he knew he had to try.

*   *   *

Jim Stinson halted his dapple brown horse on the crest of the hill and could see buildings and chimney smoke among a dark belt of pine trees about half a mile ahead. He was sick of camp food and looking forward to a meal untainted by the efforts of himself or his partner. In his mid twenties, medium height and of wiry build he resembled many of the young men who were flooding into the Black Hills, but he was not after gold. He was looking for a man, a man that he was prepared to kill. The late-model Winchester repeater in the loop on his saddle horn and the new Colt .45 on his hip advertised that his quest was far from a peaceful one.

Barney Olsen came up beside him on a big Appaloosa puddin' foot followed by their ever-reliable pack mule. A couple of years older than Jim, Barney was broader and heavier and where Jim's hair was dark, Barney's was straw-coloured as was his luxuriant moustache. But he was dressed in similar horseman's clothing and had the same armaments as his companion.

'Stopped to give that fancy-steppin' cayuse a breather?' Barney asked with a grin. He knew that Jim was very proud of his good horse and enjoyed teasing his friend. 'You should ride a decent horse that can carry a bit of weight. This one of mine will take all the weight you can pile on him and will go all day.'

'As long as you don't try to hurry him,' the other replied seriously. He had no sense of humour when his much-prized horse was disparaged. Then he pointed. 'That's White Rock up ahead.'

Barney studied the scene for a while. 'I wonder if we'll find Mason there. I'm mighty sick of lookin' for that red-headed runt. We've followed him from Kansas and must be due to catch up with him soon.'

'Catching him is only half the job. We have to try to recover the money he stole from our folks in San Matteo Valley. They trusted him to take that herd to Abilene for them but nobody was expecting him to skip with the proceeds of the sale. Now there's four families there counting on us to get back in enough time to stop the banks foreclosing on their ranches.'

'You have to hand it to the little skunk. Stealin' money is easier than stealin' its value in branded cattle. There ain't no brands on money, it travels faster and is easier to hide.'

'He was smart, that's for sure. He paid off the trail hands in Abilene so that everything seemed normal. It was a couple of weeks before our folks and the others who put together the herd, started wondering why the money had not shown up.'

They urged their mounts into motion again and Barney expressed the doubt that nagged both of them, 'I still wonder if we are really on Mason's trail. It was only luck that we found that bartender in Wichita who knew him. He reckoned Mason was talkin' of headin' for the Black Hills. But what if he was wrong, or Mason deliberately told him that to lay a false trail?'

'That's not the only worry, If he's in the Black Hills with all that stolen money, he could be looking to buy into a mine but men with no money also go there. What if he has lost or spent all our folks' money?'

'I reckon we won't know until we catch up with that sneakin', red-haired little sonofabitch — if we ever do catch up with him. But if we do and he's lost that money, I intend shootin' him to prevent further strayin' from the path of the righteous.'

'There's something else I just thought of. Someone else might rub him out first. What if he should meet up with another crook like himself or even Indians? Crazy Horse or some of the other war chiefs are not too impressed about prospectors moving into the Black Hills. There are plenty of Sioux, Cheyenne and Arapaho around these parts who would like a nice red scalp. If they get Mason before we do, all trace of that money will disappear.'

'Whatever the Sioux did would be too good for that thievin' sonofabitch. Now let's see what the folks remember about him in this town.'

White Rock scarcely qualified as a town. It was a collection of hastily built structures interspersed with rickety corrals, tents and parked wagons divided centrally by a broad dusty trail forming a street of sorts. It was the kind of place where many passed through and might pause for supplies but few lived permanently. Some newcomers and transients were still living in tents. A few constructions were built with tent roofs, half-cabin walls and were only slightly better than tents for the harsh winters like the one that had just ended.

Frontiersmen in buckskin rubbed shoulders with miners, teamsters, woodcutters and a few farming types. There were townsmen too, wearing clothes that seemed ill-designed for the rugged country around them. But women, children, churches and schools, the first signs of civilization were not yet apparent. White Rock would be as easy to tear down as it was to build.

Forever hungry and also sick of camp cooking, Barney quickly sighted a half-built cabin with a large tent attached. Red painted letters on a piece of board read; 'Buffalo's Meals'.

'Our luck's in, Jim. At least we can get somethin' between our belt buckles and our backbones without having to cook it ourselves. I could eat a horse.'

'Chances are that's what we could be eating. From what I can see this town doesn't have a butcher. Maybe it's like the sign says. Buffaloes only eat grass.'

A massive, shaggy bearded character with a shock of long black hair greeted the pair when they entered the tent. It only needed a pair of horns and he would have borne a passing resemblance to a bull buffalo. He frowned a little as he saw they were carrying their Winchesters. 'I hope you boys ain't planning a stick-up.'

'You don't need to worry on that score,' Barney told him. 'But we ain't fools enough to leave these good rifles outside on our horses and expect them to be there when we came out again.'

The man glanced at the rifles. 'Are they the 'seventy three model?'

'Sure are,' Barney said. 'They take a centrefire cartridge and hit a lot harder than the first Winchester rimfires. The centrefires are more reliable than rimfires too; the shells can be reloaded and misfires don't seem to happen now.'

'That's good. What are you boys eating? We have salt beef and potatoes or venison stew with rice and onions. And you must try my coffee. It's the best west of the Missouri. It's free with every meal.'

Both men ordered stew and each put away a generous helping but the coffee left its drinkers with the impression that someone could have been washing dogs in it. When they were leaving later the proprietor asked, 'How did you like the coffee?' Then before the others could think of a diplomatic reply he said proudly, 'It's my own secret recipe. When I was first starting business I made some for a college professor. He praised it so much that I never changed the way I made it ever since.'

'I ain't had much education,' Barney admitted, 'so maybe my tastes are different. Just how did that college fella describe your coffee?'

'I think the word he used was 'excremental' or something like that. We don't use such fancy words here but my coffee sure impressed that fella.'

'I reckon he summed it up pretty well,' Jim said. He was halfway to the door when he had a thought, 'I don't suppose you've seen a little red-haired character named Mason around here?'

'I don't know his name but a *hombre* like that came through here a couple of days ago. He was working for Herb Andrews. Herb was doing a bit of surveying up north of here. There's talk of putting in a proper road to the new diggings. They have to find a better way than the present one that crosses Cedar Creek four times in three miles.'

'Do you know where the survey camp is?' Jim tried to avoid sounding too excited.

'Not really but Zeke Danby knows. You'll probably find him over the road at Murphy's bar at this time of day. Zeke guided Andrews out to where he is camped. It's well away from the regular trail.'

'Thanks for the help. We'll tell plenty of folks about that coffee,' Barney said.

Out in the street he turned to his companion. 'It looks like we have that sneaky sonofabitch at last.'

Jim was not quite so optimistic. 'With the money that Mason stole, why would he need to work?'

2

Murphy's bar was the biggest building in White Rock; a broad-fronted, single-storey arrangement of log construction. The low, shingle roof made it dark inside but the visitors could see a tall, thin man behind the bar and a bearded man in fringed buckskins seated at a nearby table.

'Howdy boys,' the barman greeted. 'We have whiskey, whiskey and whiskey, name your poison.'

'You must have read our minds,' Jim told him. 'We'll have whiskey.' Then he turned to the man at the table. 'Is it safe to drink?'

The seated one's hairy features split into a smile. 'It ain't killed me yet but some mornings I got the feeling that it went mighty close.' He took in their clothes and asked, 'What's a couple of cow hands doin' here? Sick of chasin' cows and thinkin' of doin' a bit of prospectin' maybe?'

'No, we're looking for a man. Four families from San Matteo Creek in Texas paid a no-good by the name of Warren Mason to take a trail herd north. He sold the cattle, paid off the hands and then disappeared with the money. Our families and the other rightful owners never heard from him again. You could say that he has a bit of explaining to do. You might have seen him around these parts, a smallish, red-haired *hombre* with a weasel face — was rather partial to a drink.'

'You ain't lawmen or somethin'?'

'No, just cowmen. I'm Jim and this is Barney.'

'Pleased to meet you. I'm Zeke. Take a seat. It's been a while since I talked to someone not interested in gold.'

'They can have it,' Barney said as he took a chair. 'Diggin' around in the dirt ain't any sort of life. What do you do for a livin'?'

Zeke took a sip of his drink. 'I used

to scout for the army but these days my heart ain't in it. I can't look the Indians in the eye any more. The white men have flooded into the Black Hills and the Fort Laramie Treaty has been just about ripped up. The Indians have been sold out and I don't want to be a part of what's happenin' now. Crazy Horse was right not to put his mark on that treaty. I was making two dollars a day with meals and found provided but right now I reckon I'm between careers. Mostly I make a livin' bringin' in game for Buffalo's eatery and do a few odd jobs. But I won't scout for the army again. A couple of days ago I guided a survey team up north. They are spyin' out the possibilities of a new road but there's still some doubt about whether wagons will get through. Your red-haired friend might be with that outfit. I recall one of them was a little fella with red hair but I didn't have much to do with them. Most of the time I was scoutin' around the party lookin' for Indian sign.'

'Did you find any?' Barney asked.

'I found plenty but only huntin' parties. That place is off the reservation but the Lakota tribes are allowed to hunt there under the treaty terms. Talk is, though, that the government is gonna stop that. They intend pennin' the Indians on the reservations so that they can call hostile and shoot any they find off it. Crazy Horse and a lot like him are roamin' around off the reservation so the army figures, if they pen up the peaceful ones, they can shoot down the rest.'

Jim asked, 'How safe are those surveyors? From what I've seen an Indian in the right can kill you just as dead as one in the wrong.'

Zeke leaned back in his chair. 'Fairly safe — I spread word around the agency Indians that they were not miners and were just mappin' some of the area. I thought it best not to say that they had a road in mind. Roads bring soldiers and forts. The Indians learned that from the Bozeman trail.

Trouble's easy to find these days. There's a risk even around here and folks have been killed while campin' on the edge of town.'

'You must have a fair bit of influence with the Indians,' Barney observed.

'For ten years I worked tryin' to keep the soldiers and the Lakota from killin' each other so I got to know a lot of Indians. But I made my share of enemies too. At present, my enemies probably outnumber my friends. My life's sure going through some changes. It's hard work tryin' to work out what's best.'

Barney had little patience with the former scout's soul searching and asked, 'How would we get to this survey camp?'

'There's a fairly well defined trail headin' north from here and after about an hour's ride you'll see where the survey party turned off on the left-hand side and swung north-west. They had about a dozen mules that they were ridin' and packin'. Their trail's easy to see. It's a full day's ride so, if you intend goin' there, you'd best stay the night here and head out in the mornin'.'

'Sounds like a good idea,' Jim said. 'Is there a good place to camp around here?'

Zeke waved his right arm in a vague northerly direction. 'There's a good grassy flat on the creek about half a mile from town with plenty of firewood. Just follow the trail north out of town. Most folks camp there. Or you can camp in town over by Dawson's corrals but in that case you'll need to buy fodder for your animals.'

'We have to watch our pennies so I guess we'll camp out at the flat where our horses can eat for free.'

'That ain't the place where the Indians killed them folks you mentioned, is it?' Barney seemed to be having second thoughts.

'It is but I still have a few friends among the tribes and they reckon the hostiles are miles away to the north.

21

Since the killin's last year the army patrols this area regularly now. I'm tryin' to keep an ear to the ground so I know what's happenin' in both camps but it ain't gettin' any easier. There's whites who call me a renegade and there's Indians who don't trust me because I was once an army scout. It's mighty hard bein' in the middle when both sides are gettin' ready for war.'

'Good luck to you if you keep things peaceful,' Barney said, 'but I think you're in for a disappointment.'

Jim put down his glass. 'Thanks for the advice, Zeke. Could we buy you a drink?'

The man in buckskin looked tempted but thought better of it. 'No thanks. I'm goin' out later to see if I can get a deer. Buffalo wants one for his business. I want to make sure I can still shoot straight.'

Jim and Barney left the bar, collected their animals and rode out to the campsite that the scout had suggested. It was ideal for their purposes and they had faith in Zeke's opinion that the place was safe. With the stock watered and hobbled on good grass, the two set about preparing their camp. Both were collecting firewood when they heard a horse approaching from the north.

Barney dumped a load of wood near where they intended to make their fire and looked toward the sound. 'Someone's in a hell of a hurry,' he observed.

Seconds later a horseman emerged from around a bend in the trail. The horse was covered in foam and the rider was hunched over its neck urging every ounce of speed from it. When he saw the two campers he turned the horse toward them and hauled it to a stop a few yards away.

'Indians,' he panted. 'They just about wiped out a surveying party up on Antler Creek. My partner's bringing in the only one that got away. He sent me ahead to get help.'

'Are the Indians after him?' Jim asked, looking up the trail as he did so.

The man had calmed down slightly

23

and dismounted to ease his weary horse. 'Don't rightly know,' he admitted. 'They weren't when I left but that don't mean they ain't about. We found a young fella on the trail about an hour ago. He was done in from walking. My partner, Vern sent me ahead to get help. He's bringing the boy in slow on his horse. The kid's mighty shocked but he reckons that the rest of the party were all killed yesterday.'

The newcomer introduced himself as Homer Hopkins. He and his partner Vern Jennings were prospectors. They were on their way to the goldfields but had seen where the surveyors had turned off the trail. They started following the party's tracks to what they thought might have been a new trail to a gold strike.

'You head down to White Rock,' Jim told Hopkins, 'and see what sort of help you can arrange. Barney and I will wait here for your friend. He won't be far behind you and if we hear shooting we'll try to get to him. Tell the town folks there that we could need a bit of help if any shots are heard. We'll also join any posse that's going to the surveyors' camp later.'

'Thanks for volunteerin',' Barney grumbled. Secretly he agreed with the idea but liked to tease his partner.

'Keep an eye out for Vern. Don't shoot him by mistake,' the miner warned as he climbed back on his pony.

When Hopkins departed, the pair acted quickly. They caught their hobbled horses and pack mule, removed the hobbles and tied the animals to trees with lariats. Then they selected a position behind a big log that allowed them to cover the trail and guard the stock. There they waited.

Without taking his eyes from the landscape ahead, Barney said quietly 'We ain't never gonna get our folks' money back if the Sioux have killed Mason. Ain't a livin' soul could say what he did with it.'

'If it is him there might be something among the stuff that the Sioux left.

They won't carry off paper money. We have to know one way or another if he really is dead. But I just thought of something else: suppose the Sioux let that kid get away on purpose and are using the camp and the bodies as bait. They could be setting a trap for us when we get there.'

'I thought of that too. Maybe the folks back in town are thinkin' the same thing. They might decide to leave the job to the army if and when they come through here. Zeke might be able to give them the best advice on what to do. He'd have to know injuns pretty well.'

Jim suddenly touched Barney on the arm. 'Look at Jethro,' he whispered.

Their mule was standing with his long ears pricked, looking up the trail. The light was fading fast but the animal's nostrils were quivering as he picked up a scent of some kind. The horses were looking too.

'Someone's coming down the trail,' Jim raised his Winchester to his shoulder as he spoke. 'It might be that other prospector or it could be Indians. The trouble is that this light will make it hard to know who it is until they're dangerously close.'

Barney said nothing but pointed. Across the clearing that they were covering something indistinct was moving toward them.

Both men cocked their rifles and, in the poor light, tried to arrange their sights on what was gradually taking shape as a horse and rider. They hoped it was the second prospector and the boy but it could also have been a Sioux scout on the trail of Hopkins.

3

Outlines became clearer resolving into definite shapes and the watchers saw a man on foot leading a pack mule and a horse with a rider slumped in the saddle.

'Vern Jennings,' Jim called. 'Is that you?'

'It's me. Who are you?'

'Barney Olsen and Jim Stinson. Your partner Hopkins said you'd be along.'

'I'm mighty glad to see you. For the last hour I've been jumping at every strange sound and expecting to see Crazy Horse himself on my tracks. This is Henry Rhodes on my horse. I guess Hopkins told you about him. He's worn out and shocked pretty badly.'

Barney suggested, 'You might want to rest a while. White Rock's just down the trail a bit but you look done in.'

Jennings looked up to the boy on the

horse and said gently, 'You can get down for a spell now, Henry. You're safe here.'

Like someone in a trance the boy slid from the saddle. Jennings caught his arm and steadied him in case he fell. 'You're safe now, Henry.'

'We're not safe,' the boy said wildly. 'There's Indians everywhere . . . They might be following me . . . They'll kill us all.'

'They won't come this close to town,' Barney said and fervently hoped that he was right.

The rattle of a wagon coming from the direction of White Rock cut short any further discussion. As the men watched, an animal loped into sight. A dark-coated beast with a few white markings, it slowed to a trot when it saw the group ahead.

'It's a dog of some kind,' Jennings said.

Jim peered into the gloom. 'I think it's a greyhound. I've seen the odd one but there ain't a lot of them around these parts.'

A rattling, jingling, light wagon with a square canvas top and a pair of smartly trotting mules was not far behind the dog. Two people were on the driver's seat.

The dog saw the waiting men and trotted across to them. The wagon driver swung his team toward them and brought the vehicle to a halt.

Barney nudged Jim. 'There's a lady there.'

As if to confirm the fact, a female voice called to the dog, 'Come here, Cassius.' The dog walked back and stood by the wagon but continued to watch the men on the ground.

The man was of average appearance, somewhere in his mid-thirties, clean-shaven, and wearing town clothes but a wide-brimmed hat and a good pair of boots that showed that he knew the practicalities of frontier life.

It was his companion who commanded the most attention. The woman looked to be a bit younger, and had a pretty face framed by dark-brown curly hair.

Her clothes, though plain, showed off her neat figure to perfection.

'I'm Doctor Brophy,' the driver announced. 'I heard in White Rock that you might have a patient for me. This is my wife, Angela.'

Hats came off and the men mumbled the usual greetings. Then Jennings got down to the business at hand. 'Young Henry here's got badly blistered feet and he's had the hell — , sorry Mrs Brophy . . . scared out of him. He ain't himself yet.'

The woman laughed. 'Hell is a matter of theology or possibly geography. It's not a swear word and I've heard a lot worse.'

'By the way you talk Mrs Brophy, you ain't from around these parts.' Barney made no attempt to conceal his curiosity.

'That's right, I'm from London. Four years ago I met Nelson, my husband when he was on a visit to England. He told me about this country and here we are. Once a month we do a tour of

31

some of the smaller settlements where no doctors are available.'

While speaking, Angela climbed down from the wagon. She took the boy by the arm and, speaking gently to him, steered him to the back of the vehicle. Jim had already anticipated her moves and hurried to let down the tailboard. Together they helped the patient to a bed made up in the body of the wagon.

The doctor joined them there. 'Just take it easy and don't worry,' he told Henry. 'I'll patch you up properly back at White Rock.'

As he re-fastened the tailboard, Jim said. 'It might be an idea to get out of here quick. There could still be a few unwelcome visitors. Some folks say that Indians don't fight at night but they do if it suits them. I thought someone from town would have come out here with you.'

'Mr Hopkins was getting some help together but we thought it might be best to get out to our patient as quickly as we could. This place is close enough to town for people to hear gunfire, I'm sure that help would be sent if shooting started.'

'You have more faith in folks than I have,' Jim told him. 'And I sure wouldn't bring a lady out here tonight.'

Brophy laughed. 'It would take a braver man than I to attempt leaving her behind. Angela can be very determined.'

Barney added a warning. 'Don't give Henry any of that Buffalo *hombre's* coffee. It's like to kill him.'

Doc Brophy laughed as he helped his wife back onto the wagon seat. 'He keeps asking me what excremental means but I don't have the heart to shatter his illusions. Jennings said to tell you that he will try to get a few men together tomorrow and go up to that survey camp. He would appreciate all the help he can get.'

'Tell him we'll talk it over in town tonight,' Jim told him. 'After you go, we'll move our camp back to town.'

Less than a hundred yards away a

buckskin-clad figure stole away on moccasined feet. He dared not come closer in case the animals picked up his scent but his keen ears had heard all that he needed to know.

★ ★ ★

They set out before sunrise, seven men well-armed and mounted. Zeke led the way and Jim, Barney and two miners, Rowley and Myers rode together. Jennings and Hopkins brought up the rear.

Rowley had been an army officer during the Civil War and assumed the leadership of the group. He was a big man, somewhere in his forties with a bushy black beard. His saddle was an old Grimsley design which he sat awkwardly because of a serious leg wound he had suffered. His right foot stuck out at a sharp angle and his body was twisted in the saddle.

'He'd be hell on horses' backs, sittin' crooked like that,' Barney whispered to Jim.

Rowley had a booming voice, a legacy of shouting orders to an artillery battery and could be heard a considerable distance away.

As discreetly as he could, Zeke warned him about speaking too loudly. 'It's quiet out here and human voices carry a long way. We don't want to attract any Sioux that could be roamin' about.'

The big man remembered for a few minutes but gradually he forgot and his voice became louder again. Zeke was far from happy with the situation but volunteers for the party had been hard to get. Rowley had a good reputation though as a fighting man so that was some consolation. The scout had no idea of the fighting ability of the others.

'I'll go a couple of hundred yards ahead and look for signs,' Zeke announced. 'Keep me in sight. Watch our flanks too in case they hit us from the side. In this country they can slip around a scout who's in front.'

'Are you expecting them to?' Jim asked.

'You can only expect the unexpected with Indians. I can't see everywhere at once. You fellas keep your eyes open too.'

As the scout cantered out ahead Barney turned to Jim. 'I reckon Zeke really knows this business.'

'He does,' Myers interjected, 'but some reckon he's too close to the Indians. From what he says sometimes it's hard to know what side he's really on but if I wasn't prepared to trust him, I wouldn't be here.'

As the sun rose higher, conversation dried up. Even Rowley fell silent. The route lay through rolling country with patches of pine on some hills and willows and cottonwoods beside the small creek to the right of the trail. A line of distinctive buttes lay ahead while to the west, individual low hills gradually gave way to mountain ranges.

At noon they found a shady clump of cottonwoods where they rested for a while, removing the bits from the horses' mouths to enable them to graze.

Jim and Zeke kept watch while the others relaxed. But while watching or resting all chewed on sandwiches that Buffalo had donated as his contribution to the expedition. He had offered a canteen of his special coffee but Zeke told him that they were travelling light and did not want extra weight on their horses. They could make do with creek water until they returned to town.

The scene was so peaceful that the grim reality of the men's task was momentarily forgotten until Zeke called out, 'Look at those buttes.'

All eyes turned northwards to view the broken column of white smoke rising from the flat top of one of the buttes.

'I don't like the look of that,' Jim observed. Then he asked Zeke where the Indians were in relation to their destination.

'The survey camp is a couple of miles to the left of that smoke.'

'About where *that* smoke is?' Barney pointed to another signal now rising

37

from a mountain on their left.

Hopkins swore. Even Rowley fell silent and looked worried.

Jennings asked, 'Can you read what that smoke says?'

'It's not like writin',' Zeke explained. 'The meanin' of the signals is agreed upon beforehand. Only those the smoke is intended for know what it means. It might have nothin' to do with us. Scattered huntin' parties sometimes keep in touch with each other that way.'

'They might be hunting parties,' Hopkins said as he watched the smoke, 'but I have the feeling that they are hunting us. How far are we from Andrews' camp?'

The scout pointed to some tiny black dots in the sky. 'Those birds are buzzards. The camp is only an hour's ride from here. I reckon it's right under them buzzards.'

'That puts it midway between those signals,' Jim frowned deeply as he spoke. He was far from comfortable with the situation that was unfolding.

With growing unease the party continued their journey. All were determined to fulfil their mission but none was happy about their chances of avoiding trouble.

'I know a few of the Sioux,' Zeke said. 'If I get the chance I might be able to talk us out of trouble.'

'If you get the chance,' Myers growled.

This time the scout did not ride so far ahead and thus reduced the risk of being cut off from the others. An air of nervousness pervaded the group and a higher degree of vigilance became evident.

'I saw something,' Hopkins suddenly called. He reined in his horse and pointed to a brush-covered hillside. The others looked, but the only movement was the brush that a slight wind was stirring.

'Are you sure you ain't seeing things?' Jennings said as he studied the hillside.

'I saw something. It was only a quick

39

glimpse but something was moving on the side of that hill.'

'It could have been a deer or a bear or even a mountain lion,' Barney suggested.

'Maybe. But whatever it was, it sort of moved like a man.' The prospector was not convinced.

Zeke saw them, halted and cantered back. He too looked, saw nothing and suggested that they waste no more time. Just over a ridge ahead, he told them, was the creek that would lead them to the survey camp. 'It ain't far to go now. Let's do what we came for as quick as we can and get to hell out of here. I don't want to be around these parts one second longer than I need to be.'

Rowley glanced at the hills around. 'So you're expecting trouble?'

'There's a mighty good chance of it,' the scout grunted.

4

The scene at the camp fulfilled their worst expectations. Scavengers had been at work on the bodies; the buzzards were reluctant to leave their grim repast and the men dared not scatter them with a gunshot. By throwing sticks and stones at them, they finally forced away the sluggish, bloated birds. The attackers had plundered the site and anything they could not use was broken, torn, or scattered around the area.

Zeke waved an arm toward the scene. 'There it is, gents. Do what you have to do and get out as quick as you can. I'll leave all the hard work to you. I'm gonna ride around and make sure our feathered friends ain't creepin' up on us. Holler as soon as you're ready to go again.'

'Where do we even start with a mess

like this?' Hopkins said as he dismounted and hitched his horse to a tree.

'I suppose our first job is to identify who these people are,' Jim suggested.

Barney agreed. 'Jim and I might know one of them.'

'I know, or I did know Andrews,' Rowley said.

Myers was never a man to waste words. 'Good luck — not even their mothers would know them now.'

The Sioux had not carried away the camp's crowbar or shovels so the miners took these, selected a spot for a mass grave and started digging. This left the others with the stomach-churning task of collecting the mutilated bodies. Much as cow hands dislike shovels, Jim and Barney would have happily traded places with the grave diggers as they started their gruesome work. One after another they lined up the bodies at the grave site.

A discarded notebook contained some of the survey camp's details and expenses. Names and wages due were also listed there. Rowley took the book and stuffed it into the side pocket of his coat. He was able to identify Andrews but there was a certain amount of guesswork about the others.

The name Mason was not listed in the notebook but that did not surprise Jim and Barney. What remained of the red-haired man was approximately the right size for the one they were after but his features were unrecognizable.

'Do you think that's him?' Jim asked.

Barney was not sure. 'Most likely, but I can't say for certain. If it is, it served that thieving coyote right. If that really is Mason we have no hope now of gettin' the folks' money back. We might have to start thinkin' of headin' for home.'

The burial was a hasty one. Rowley stammered through a half-remembered prayer as the others filled in the grave.

Then all retired to the nearby creek to drink and wash themselves.

'That Rhodes kid was mighty lucky,'

43

Hopkins said as he looked at the low creek bank. 'He didn't have much to hide behind here.'

'I doubt he'll ever get that lucky again,' Rowley said as he dried his hands on the seat of his pants.

A rifle shot sounded from the other side of the hill, then another.

'Zeke's in trouble,' Jim called. 'Get to the horses.'

They ran quickly to their mounts and wasted no time getting into the saddle. Another shot sounded.

Zeke came over the crest of the hill riding hard. 'Get goin'!' he shouted. 'They're right behind me.'

As if to emphasize the danger, there were a couple more shots and Myers reeled in his saddle.

Jim spurred alongside, caught the wounded man and pushed him upright again. 'Grab the saddle horn and hang on,' he shouted, 'I'll lead your horse.'

'It's my arm,' the wounded man said. 'Feels like it's on fire.'

'Hang on with your good hand. If

you fall off you're gone.'

The horses were all fully into their strides now, streaking across the rough ground as though infected by their riders' fear.

Zeke slowed his mount allowing Jim and Myers to go ahead. He had a six-shooter in one hand. 'I'll try to slow them down a bit.' He wheeled his pony into a clump of pines. The others heard a flurry of revolver shots and then a rifle boomed. Rowley's horse jumped as a shot grazed it but fortunately, it stayed on its feet.

Jim glanced behind and saw Zeke riding hard some distance back. Relief swept through him because he feared that the scout had been killed.

The riders had left the hills behind and were on a broad, open plain when their fear subsided. To preserve their horses, they slowed the pace; all knew how quickly the lightly weighted Indian ponies could run down tired horses.

Barney looked behind and saw no sign of the pursuit. 'Hold up,' he shouted. 'They've stopped chasin' us.'

Gradually the pace slowed and eventually the whole party halted. They clustered around the wounded man, trying to stop the bleeding while causing as little pain as possible to a broken forearm. The attention was hasty and painful but eventually the wound was bandaged and the arm tucked inside the miner's shirtfront. He was nauseous and would have liked to rest a while but Jim discouraged that idea.

'Best keep moving, but hold the pace down to a walk. That run took a lot out of these horses.' He pointed to the red furrow across the rump of Rowley's big sorrel. 'That's only a graze but the horse could stiffen up and go lame as it cools. Standing around might not do it a lot of good and we don't want to be too close to the Sioux if we are forced to stop later.'

It was a much more relieved group who continued their journey. They needed no convincing that they had been lucky.

'You were the right man in the right place for us back there,' Jim said to Zeke as their horses were walking abreast. 'How many Indians do you reckon you saw?'

'I didn't stop to count them but there were too many for us and they were in no mood to talk. But I would not go into this area again until the army drives all the hostiles out of it.'

'I thought you reckoned the Indians had gotten a raw deal and you didn't want the army around.'

'You're right. I would be happy if the Sioux and Cheyenne kept all white men out of here, specially gold miners. They are greedy sonsabitches. I'm just sayin' that the army will have to clear the hostiles out of here before it's safe for white men to go back, but I ain't in favour of that happenin'. We were lucky not to lose our scalps back there — this is still Indian land in my book.'

★ ★ ★

Angela walked out of the tent that was their temporary home when her husband did his monthly circuit of the isolated settlements. Henry Rhodes was seated on the tongue of their wagon idly stroking her dog's head. The boy was slowly recovering from his experience but still seemed more at ease with the dog than he was with people; Cassius asked no questions and did not remind him of the horror he had seen.

She joked, 'You and Cassius seem to be deep in conversation there, Henry.'

For the first time the boy smiled. 'He's a nice dog. I never heard of a dog named Cassius before.'

'He was named after Shakespearse's Cassius with the lean and hungry look.'

'That Shakespeare fellow must not have fed his dogs too well. This one's in great condition.'

'He wasn't when we got him. He was a scrawny, neglected little pup.'

'I don't know how I can pay you and the doc for the way you've looked after me. You've patched up my feet and fed

48

me and let me sleep in your wagon. Andrews never got a chance to pay us any wages. I was only three days into the job when the Indians came.'

'Don't worry about that now. Nelson and I will be waiting around to see if he's needed when the men get back from the camp.'

The haunted look returned to Henry's face. 'They might not come back. There's too many Indians up there. They were crazy to go.'

'This time they have Zeke Danby with them and are ready for trouble. They won't be caught by surprise. But meanwhile I have just thought of something you might do for us. Would you groom and feed our two mules? They are over there in Dawson's corrals behind Buffalo's establishment. Nelson has to see a couple of people this afternoon but if you look after the mules, I can do a bit of painting. There is a nice little spot down by the creek that could be the subject of a nice landscape if I can do it justice.'

Henry's worried look returned. 'I'll fix the mules but don't go too far away on your own, Mrs Brophy. Those Indians can come right close to town sometimes. It could be dangerous. I heard Mr Andrews say that they had killed people within sight of here.'

'Don't worry, Henry. I have been out west long enough to know what's dangerous. I have a small revolver in my paint box and Cassius suspects all Indians as well as being able to detect other suspicious characters. He is a great bodyguard.'

'You be careful, Mrs Brophy. This isn't England. There's lots can go wrong here.'

'Stop worrying, Henry. I won't be taking any risks. I've lived in this country long enough to know not to be foolish.'

'Some folks have plenty of experience but bad luck can happen. Please be careful.'

5

Angela took her painting equipment, called to Cassius and walked to a small grassy flat within sight of the town. It was a pretty spot that she felt urged to paint. The flat sloped gradually to a shallow, stony part of the small, clear creek. Beyond the stream was a tangle of dark green brush around the base of a colourful, red-and-yellow-streaked, rocky bluff. The afternoon sun was hitting the water at just the right angle and as she planned out her picture, her biggest worry was the best way to depict the sparkle of the water.

The dog explored a few rabbit burrows on the flat but did not wander too far from its mistress. When it tired of this pastime, it would seek a shady spot close to where Angela was working and stretch out as though asleep, but one cocked ear showed that he was still keeping guard.

The painting was progressing better than she had anticipated and she paid little attention to time. She might have been there for an hour or even longer when Cassius came to his feet in a swift, easy motion. His owner took little notice as he trotted down to the edge of the stream and stood with ears pricked, staring at the brush on the other side. Then he barked and gave a low growl that announced the presence of an intruder.

It could have been a fox, or a coyote or some other animal so at first Angela took little notice. But then the barking became more urgent. Whatever was over the stream was not running away. Something in the brush did not fear a large, suspicious dog.

'Cassius, come here.' She had seen bears before and knew that the shallow stream would be no barrier at all to a charging grizzly. Again she called the dog.

It backed away reluctantly, still barking and growling and watching the brush. The tops of the bushes were moving halfway up the hill and the movement caught her eye. For a fraction of a second, something red showed through a small break in the foliage.

Suddenly Angela remembered what Henry had told her about people on the edge of town being snatched by Indians. She opened the paint box and took out the small .32 revolver but then realized the limits of its range and power. Leaving her work where it was, she called the dog to her side. 'Good boy, Cassius, we're going back to Nelson, now.'

★ ★ ★

It was dark when the party returned from the survey camp. Doc Brophy heard them arriving and hurried out of the tent to see if they needed his help. They certainly did because Myers was in intense pain as well as being physically exhausted by his long ride.

Jim and Barney had decided to stay the night in town and were arranging further accommodation and feed for their animals with Harry Dawson who owned the corrals. The retired teamster had realized that the many travellers to the goldfields were happy to pay for a safe place to leave their stock overnight and did not mind paying a small amount for the convenience.

Dawson agreed with the pair that they were safer staying in town for the night. 'There could be Indians about. Someone gave Doc Brophy's wife a good scare while you were away today.'

'Was she hurt?' Barney asked.

'No. She was painting a picture just down by the creek and figgered there was someone hiding in the brush on the other side. She had sense enough to leave her painting and get out of there. The doc and a couple of men went back later to collect her paints and things. There were moccasin tracks. It looked like two Indians had a look at the painting and left the area. They probably figured that someone might be back with a few guns.'

'Do hostile Sioux come this close to town very often?' Jim was surprised because he thought that roving war parties would not be likely to advertise their presence.

'It happens, though it's mostly on the other side of town. A few men coming back from the goldfields have been ambushed fairly close to here. Seems like they followed them out of the badlands and surprised them when they thought they were safe. Them travellers got scalped and cut up pretty bad. We never could find out who some of them were.'

Later that evening the pair met the Brophys at Buffalo's restaurant. They exchanged pleasantries and then Jim inquired about Myers.

'The arm's badly broken,' Doc Brophy told him. 'But I hope that it will get right.'

Barney said to Angela, 'I hear that the Sioux or Cheyenne gave you a scare today, Mrs Brophy.'

'I had an anxious moment or two but Cassius warned me in time. There were tracks of two different pairs of moccasins. The men who saw them all said they were made by Indians but I'm not so sure. Some white men, specially hunting types wear moccasins too. They must have been art lovers because they did not take my painting.'

Her husband laughed. 'I can't imagine Crazy Horse hanging too many paintings on the wall of his tepee, dear.'

'You can laugh, Nelson but I don't think that those men were Indians at all. There were a lot of different coloured paints left behind. I doubt that a wild Indian would be able to resist such a variety of colours. They would have made him the most colourful warrior on the warpath.'

'You have a good point there, Mrs Brophy,' Jim said. 'I agree with you. Most Indians I have seen would not be able to resist those pretty colours.'

Her husband offered another theory.

'We might be over dramatizing the whole thing. Some of these backwoods types are not at ease around women. They might have been watching out of curiosity and might not have meant any harm.'

'Does Zeke know about this?' Barney asked.

The doctor replied, 'I mentioned it to him when they brought in Myers. He thought we should stay close to town until he has had a chance to look around.'

'He saved us today. If Zeke hadn't been keepin' an eye out, we would have all lost our hair up at the surveyors' camp.'

Jim agreed. 'We used up our share of luck today. Myers was ahead of Barney and me when we skedaddled out of there. The bullet that hit him must have gone between us and it was the same with the one that grazed Rowley's horse. Some of those shots would have gone mighty close to Zeke too. He was closer to the Indians than any of us.'

Barney stood up, stretched and yawned. 'Sorry to bust up the party, folks but I need some sleep. It's been a long day.'

Jim also pushed back his chair. 'I'd better go too. I can see Buffalo over there with a coffee pot. He's likely to bring some more if we hang around.'

White Rock had no such thing as street lighting. Patches of lamplight escaping from windows threw illuminated patches on the ground but mostly the single street was dark with holes and ridges making walking hazardous. Both men stumbled and cursed their way to their campsite near Dawson's corrals.

They rolled out their bedrolls on a level piece of ground not far from the corrals, removed boots, hats and gunbelts and took their firearms under the blankets away from the rusting night air. Minutes later both were asleep.

It was a disturbance in the corral that woke Jim, a nervous trampling and snorting. Worried that a couple of animals might have been fighting, he threw the blankets aside, pulled on his boots and walked to the corral. If he could find the troublesome animal he intended to move it to another corral before it kicked and crippled one of the others. The animals were milling about nervously and had raised a certain amount of dust that hung in the air like mist.

Jim spoke quietly so that the stock would not be startled by his sudden appearance. 'What's the matter with you knot heads?'

The answer to his question came in the form of a dark figure that detached itself from beside a big corner post and came charging at him. Something shiny showed in the attacker's right hand and it swept upwards, aimed at the startled cowhand's mid-section.

It was only a reflex action that swung Jim's left arm inside his opponent's knife hand and their forearms collided solidly stopping the knife short of its intended target. A powerful, instinctively thrown, right-hand punch landed on the assailant's chin and the dark shape reeled away but the man was not down and the knife was still in his hand. To move closer would bring him back into knife range. Hoping to forestall another onslaught, Jim lashed out with his boot landing a solid kick on the man's shin. The sharp intake of breath indicated that the attacker was hurt. But he was still on his feet and an unarmed man fighting one with a knife in the dark, was unlikely to survive for long.

Jim took to his heels. 'Barney!' he shouted as he fled, 'Indians!'

Barney, already awakened by the sounds of the scuffle, came out of his blankets with a six-gun in his hand. As his brain started taking in the scene, he saw Jim running toward him and a dark figure a couple of paces behind. He snapped a shot at the pursuer. It missed but the man turned and in a limping run, disappeared into the darkness.

'How many are there?' Barney demanded.

Jim grabbed his gunbelt before replying, 'I only saw one. I think he was trying to run off the horses but he damn near got me.'

A light showed in the window of Dawson's cabin on the other side of the corrals. 'What's happening?' a voice called.

'An Indian was tryin' to steal the horses. Be careful. There could be others around.' Barney was pulling on his boots as he answered.

'Wait till I get a gun and I'll join you.'

Armed and fully dressed once more the three men cautiously searched the area around the corrals but found nothing.

'There could be others about or this injun might really have been scalp hunting,' Dawson said. 'It might be best to spread the word around town just in case he has friends. I'll keep guard here if you boys will wander down the street and warn anyone who asks about what has happened.'

As the two younger men walked away

to begin their task, Barney started to chuckle, 'I never knew you could run so fast, Jim, and all from one Indian with one little knife.'

'I never figured you were such a bad shot, Barney. I was bringing him up to you for you to shoot him. He was a big target, and you missed.' Mid-way through their banter, Jim suddenly paused. 'I just thought. That was no Indian . . . I remember now. When I hit him I felt a beard. That was a white man.'

'Or maybe a half-breed, some of them have beards.'

'You could be right but we'd better start warning people. I can see some lamps being lit.'

★ ★ ★

Pete Gordon was nursing a sore shin and a badly cut mouth. When he took a swig of the raw whiskey he had in the tin cup, the pain was excruciating. If it had not hurt so much to speak, he would have sworn. Only when the pain subsided did he wipe his streaming eyes and glare at his two companions in their isolated mountain camp.

Idaho Taylor and Jerry Fitch knew too much to laugh at their hair-triggered companion's plight. Taylor was bigger than Gordon but had seen the latter in fights and knew that he could never match the other's ferocity.

Fitch, a little runt of a man, was not quite so scared of Gordon but preferred not to be in a situation where he had to kill him. If the chips were down, he was pretty sure that the Merwin & Hulbert revolver he carried would cancel out any disparity in size and fighting ability.

All three were dressed in buckskins and moccasins but their bearded faces prevented them from being mistaken as Indians. Taylor even affected a Mexican sombrero. They were roughly the same age, in their mid-thirties and at one time or another had lived with the Lakota tribes or worked for the army but now they had chosen a different path in life.

'It was a lousy idea,' Gordon mumbled through swollen lips. 'I damn near got shot and we didn't manage to run off those horses. It was a waste of everyone's time.'

Fitch stopped rolling his cigarette. 'No it wasn't. The horses were not important. Crooked Foot wants to keep the scare into those people in White Rock. He wants 'em good and scared and sticking close to town. From where I was with our own ponies, I could see lights going on all over town after that shot was fired. Those greenhorns will be expecting to see an Indian behind every tree.'

'They won't stay holed up forever. Sooner or later someone will find their way up to Antler Creek,' Taylor said. 'That survey party would have upset things if they had been allowed to stay there.'

'But they didn't last long there, did they?' Fitch reminded. 'Crooked Foot saw to that. If they found out anything, they can't tell anyone now.'

'What about the kid who was allowed to get away?' Gordon was not convinced that any should have been allowed to escape.

'That was smart. They had not been there long enough to learn anything and allowing one survivor to get back put a good scare into everyone else. They'll think twice before they start coming into this country again for a while.'

Gordon mumbled, 'We're playing a mighty dangerous game here and I can't see us coming out of it with too many friends.'

'That's what I reckon too,' Taylor agreed.

'You pair worry too much,' Fitch told them. 'Things are working well. In a couple of weeks, we'll be rich men. I'm getting the hell out of this country then and I don't care what happens at Antler Creek. Eventually the army and the Sioux will be killing themselves all over the place and I wouldn't give a damn if they wiped each other out.'

'Don't let Crooked Foot hear you saying things like that,' Taylor said. 'We have to stay on good terms with both sides.'

'Not for much longer. It's easy enough with the army because we have all worked with them as scouts or packers at some time or other. They trust us, but a few Lakota are getting suspicious. It's nearly time for me, Jeremiah Fitch to get out.'

Taylor had second thoughts about that. 'There's still a heap of gold there.'

'How much more do you want?' Gordon demanded. 'Already you have more than you could spend in a lifetime.'

'Not with his thirst,' Fitch laughed.

'You two can laugh but when I make my pile I might go east and marry me some pretty little girl like the one we seen painting pictures near the creek yesterday.'

'We were lucky that girl didn't start

yelling and screaming about Indians.' Gordon said. 'She was sure a cool one.'

'She wouldn't have seen us at all if Fitch had kept that red undershirt covered up like he should have. Why, when I was with Carrington on the Bozeman Trail — '

'Shut up, Idaho,' the little man interrupted. 'We needed an Indian scare and things worked out just right. Of course the scare would have been better if we could have run off those horses and mules and scalped that *hombre* who interfered, but Gordon can't help being a clumsy sonofabitch.'

The big man glared at Fitch. 'One day I'll scalp you, you scrawny little buzzard.'

'Kill each other some other time,' Taylor said in a tired voice. 'It's time we got back to work.'

* * *

White Rock did not have many hiding places but Jim and Barney were keeping low profiles in case Buffalo spotted them and bestowed his usual hospitality in the form of a free cup of coffee. The big man was gregarious by nature and enjoyed the company of any newcomers to the town who might bring news of what was happening in more interesting places.

The pair were resigned to the fact that Mason was dead and had assembled their outfit, packing up to leave. But matters were still uncertain so they decided to check the situation with Zeke before venturing from town. As they walked toward the saloon, they saw Henry Rhodes approaching. Someone had donated some ill-fitting clothes but they were clean and the boy was looking much brighter than he had been.

'Howdy, Henry,' Barney greeted. 'What are you up to today?'

'I've got me a job. Mrs Brophy arranged it for me. I cut wood and help Buffalo; he gives me bed and board and even a dollar a week. She's a great lady, Doc Brophy's wife and she's a great artist too. She was showing me some of her sketches. As well as scenery she draws pictures of Indians and all sorts of people. There was one of a soldier she did in Bismark and it was like one of them photographs. Ask her to show it to you. It's the best drawing I ever saw.'

'If I get the chance and she's not too busy, I might ask her about it,' Jim said and hoped that he had sufficiently disguised his insincerity. He had more on his mind than art work.

Barney had another idea. 'You don't help Buffalo make that coffee do you?'

Henry shook his head. 'That's a real secret. I don't think he would even tell his own mother how he makes it.'

At this point they saw Zeke walking to the saloon so they took their leave of Henry and walked over to the frontiers-man. They noticed that he was walking with a slight limp.

'Howdy Zeke,' Jim greeted. 'Looks like you're trotting a bit lame today.'

'I've been like that for years. A horse fell with me and my foot was still in the stirrup. It busted a few bones some-where but healed up in a sort of a way. Sometimes it gives me a bit of trouble though, specially in cold weather.'

Barney sympathized. 'I didn' break no bones but had a horse come down on my leg once. I couldn't believe that anything could be so heavy. Jim and I were thinking of joining you for a drink if it ain't too early in the day for you.'

'It suits me fine. Let's go.'

A few minutes later the three were seated in the bar with a bottle of whiskey and three chipped glasses between them — not many drinking glasses came up the trail to White Rock. Afer a few comments of a general nature they got down to business.

'Seems like you boys have something on your minds,' Zeke said leaning back in his chair.

Jim replied. 'You could say that. There was something a bit funny about that Indian horse raid that failed last night. The one that chased me with a knife wasn't an Indian.'

Zeke's eyes narrowed. 'What makes you think that?'

'He was big, for a start. Most Indians I've seen are not tall men and those that are, seem to be thin, wiry customers. My man was wearing buckskins and moccasins but he was white.'

'How can you be sure?'

'I felt a beard when I hit him in the face.'

'I ain't surprised. There's a lot of half-breeds with the Lakota tribes. Chances are it was one of them. Or it could be a white crook just looking to steal some horses and mules.'

'If it was a white man he was takin' a hell of a risk,' Barney observed. 'Drivin' a herd of horses, stolen or otherwise, through this country at present is invitin' an Indian attack.'

'Unless he had a special arrangement with the Sioux,' Jim suggested.

Zeke disagreed. 'Deals like that would be mighty unlikely. There was a time when I was in pretty good standing with the Sioux, but not now.

They no longer trust any white men. Chances are that last night's visitor was a half-breed living with the hostiles. I knew a few that did.'

'We were thinking of heading home,' Jim said. 'Do you reckon it's safe to take the road south?'

'I wouldn't. A few of my old friends from scouting days were telling me they had seen Indian sign on the southern road. Take my advice and sit tight here until the army sends a parol to clear the road.'

That idea did not appeal to Barney. 'What if we head north-east toward the Black Hills? There's a fair bit of traffic along that trail.'

'There is,' Zeke agreed, 'but folks going to and from the gold country are getting rubbed out on a regular basis. Stay here until you know that the trails are safe. It takes a lot to scare Doc Brophy but him and his wife ain't tempting fate. The Indians know them and they have helped some of their people in the past but chances are they could meet some mighty ungrateful strangers if they leave here too soon.'

Jim drained his glass. 'This is a mighty strange situation. You're telling us that White Rock is under siege,' he said. 'But we haven't seen an Indian around here. If they are surrounding the town, they're laying mighty low.'

Zeke smiled. 'They have a habit of doing that but Jim Bridger used to say that where you can see Indians is where they're thickest. From my experience he's right.'

'You're probably right,' Jim conceded. 'I suppose we're getting impatient to be home. We've been gone for nearly a year.'

'Look on the bright side, boys. While you're here your horses are getting rested and are putting on condition. That means you'll make better time on the trail when you start back. I suppose you have girlfriends to go back to.'

'No such luck. We'll be going back to tell four ranchin' families that we couldn't recover the money that Mason coyote stole.' Barney frowned at the thought. 'Those folks were just hangin' on. I reckon our failure will destroy them.'

'They'll be even more destroyed if you two lose your hair,' Zeke cautioned. 'Don't do anything foolish here. Just wait till the army says it's safe to travel again.'

6

'Look what's comin' down the street,' Barney said.

Rowley, the big miner had replaced his wounded horse with another and was riding ahead of a group of heavily armed horsemen. They looked like miners but each had a rifle and at least one revolver. There were six men behind the leader and all bore the determined look of men on serious business.

Rowley checked his horse in front of the two cowmen. 'Howdy, boys. We're heading up to Antler Creek. If you feel like a ride you're welcome to come along. A couple of extra guns won't go astray.'

Jim was puzzled. 'What do you reckon to be doing up there? Wasn't our last visit exciting enough for you?'

The miner leaned down and said in a

low voice, 'I want to have a good look along the creek. That looks like gold-bearing country to me but for some reason, it seems never to have been prospected.'

'There are plenty of reasons,' Barney interjected, 'and they all have feathers in their hair.'

'I know that but they won't surprise us like they did the other day. This is your chance to make a fortune. Come with us. You could be rich men in a couple of days.'

Jim was not even tempted. He had encountered optimistic prospectors before. 'Thanks for the offer, but I'll stay here.' He turned to Barney. 'What about you?'

'I reckon I'll stay here.' Then he asked Rowley, 'Did you talk over this idea with Zeke?'

'I did last night. He reckons we're crazy. But a man has to take a few risks sometimes.' Rowley gathered up his reins as he spoke and urged his horse into motion. 'I'll see you around.'

'Best of luck,' Jim said.

★ ★ ★

'You're acting very strangely today, Cassius,' Angela said to the dog. It was standing with pricked ears looking to the north-west. He whined as his owner walked across to him but seemed distracted. Normally when she was close the dog gave her his full attention. Something was wrong.

Then she remembered how the dog had acted strangely when her last painting expedition had been interrupted. There had been Indians then.

Jim and Barney saw Angela looking concerned when they emerged from Buffalo's after breakfast. 'You look worried, Mrs Brophy,' Jim said as they approached.

'It's Cassius. He's acting very strangely. He was like that when those Indians were prowling about the other day. I was wondering if some more might be lurking about.'

'I've seen dogs scared of storms that were comin' from miles away,' Barney suggested.

'There's not a cloud in the sky, Mr Olsen.' Angela still felt that she did not know the pair well enough to call them by their first names. She added, 'Cassius has never been frightened of storms anyway.'

Jim was fond of dogs and idly stroked the animal's sleek head as he looked in the same direction. 'I doubt it would be Indians. There was a bunch of armed men rode out in that direction early this morning. They were armed to the teeth and the Sioux would never get them all quietly even if — ' He paused in mid-sentence. Turning to Barney he said, 'I just thought — maybe the dog can hear shooting. Dogs' hearing is a lot better than ours. I wonder if Rowley and the others have run into trouble.'

'Do you really reckon they have?'

Jim rubbed a hand across his bristly chin as he often did when deep in thought. 'Could be. It's a good morning for a ride though. Why don't we ride out along the trail a ways and have a look, or at least, a listen?'

'It beats hangin' round town,' Barney agreed, adding, 'even if we're relyin' on a hound dog's opinion.'

Angela flushed. 'He's no ordinary dog — he's Cassius.'

The devil was in Barney. With a sly smile he said to the dog, 'What do you reckon about us goin' out to have a look around?'

As expected, the greyhound said nothing.

'I don't think he's prepared to give advice so Jim and I will just have to figure things out for ourselves.'

Angela looked concerned. 'It might be dangerous. Are you sure it's safe to go out there?'

'We won't go too far,' Jim promised. 'Just to be sure, you could tell your husband or maybe Zeke Danby where we've gone. They might want to organize some sort of defence for the town in case we're wrong.'

Barney looked at Cassius. 'You could save a lot of trouble if you could only talk.'

Angela laughed. 'He's trying to talk. It's not his fault if we don't speak his language. Do you like dogs, Mr Olsen?'

'Maybe if they were cooked right I might but the Comanches I was with at the time weren't the best of cooks.'

Angela looked horrified. 'You wouldn't eat a dog would you?'

'Certainly not a whole one, ma'am.'

Jim growled. 'If you want to get scalped before you even leave White Rock, you're going the right way about it.'

★　★　★

They were roughly two miles from town when they heard the first distant shot. There was a pause and then another report.

'That dog was right,' Barney said. 'There is shootin' up ahead of us. Sounds like someone is in trouble.'

They spurred their horses along the trail left by Rowley's men. It was easy to see and follow. Both riders were alert, listening for more shooting but hearing none above the pounding of their own horses' hoofs.

Jim pointed to a ridge ahead. 'Stop when we get there and we'll have another listen. We don't want to gallop into an ambush.'

At the top of the rise they looked out over a series of stony, red ridges partially covered with brush and pine trees. They could not see down into the shady valleys but they were close enough to hear the next flurry of shooting when it came. Several shots from different-sounding weapons were identified and they were not far away.

'Where do you reckon they're comin' from?' Barney asked.

'It's hard to tell because of the way the shots are echoing in the hollows but I reckon they're close.'

'Horses comin' and comin' fast.' Barney stood in his stirrups and peered down into the valley ahead. 'Do we run or join in?'

'Let's just get over there in the brush

and see who's doing what and how many of them there are. There's no point in biting off more than we can chew.'

Urging their horses off the trail, the pair took shelter behind the foliage of a massive blue spruce. Both drew their carbines and ensured that they were loaded. The hoofbeats were getting louder and then they heard a shot. Something white could be seen moving through the distant trees and suddenly a grey horse carrying two riders burst into view.

The man in the saddle was hatless crouched low over his mount's neck with legs flailing in an effort to wring more speed from the animal. The second rider was clinging to his companion's waist and looking fearfully back over his shoulder.

'Those are Rowley's men,' Jim told his partner.

'Just look what's behind them,' Barney said quietly. 'No wonder they're runnin'.'

7

A wild rider with feathers in his streaming black hair and paint on his face swept into view on a stretch-necked, galloping, pinto pony that was gaining on the white men at every stride. Other pursuers were also coming into view.

The man on the pinto raised a Spencer carbine as the distance between the horses closed. At that range the big Spencer bullet was quite capable of going through both men.

'Get the others!' Jim shouted as he threw his Winchester to his shoulder and fired. The 200-grain, .44 slug smashed the Indian from his pony and sent him rolling into the dust.

Barney had a good target and even though mounted on a moving horse, he was able to spray lead into the main body of the pursuers.

One rider on an iron jawed horse shot out from those around him, who were convinced they had ridden into an ambush and were hauling back on their reins. He sawed frantically at his horse's bit and a look of horror flashed over his face. Given more time he might have even thrown himself from the saddle but his time had run out. Barney's bullet hit him in the chest. He slumped, grabbed at the saddle horn and fell sideways as his horse turned away.

'That's a white man,' Jim called as he too concentrated his fire on the tangle of riders before them.

But the pursuers had suffered heavily with men and horses wounded as well as the two fatalities. Fearing that the ambushers might follow them and unsure of their numbers, they wheeled their horses about and galloped out of sight. The rapidly receding hoofbeats were a sure sign that they were not stopping to regroup.

'Let's get a quick look at those we got and then we'll try to catch up with these others.' Jim steered his horse out onto the trail as he spoke.

'Keep your gun handy in case they're playin' possum,' Barney warned.

Jim needed no convincing. 'I'll watch these. You keep an eye out in case our friends come back. There were a couple of white men or half-breeds with that bunch. Two of them were riding on saddles and Indians on the warpath don't do that. They don't trust saddles.'

He rode across to the fallen attackers, dismounted and left his horse standing, reins down, as it had been trained to stand.

The Indian was dead but Jim noticed that his hair was roached up on his head in a style he had not seen before. He was more familiar with Comanches and Kiowas but wasted no time attempting to identify the dead warrior's tribe.

The white man was still stirring and breathing hoarsely through blood-flecked lips. There was no fight left in him and he was plainly dying but Jim took the precaution of removing the stricken one's revolver before he knelt beside him. 'What's all this about?' he asked in a tone that was far from gentle.

The man on the ground seemed as though he would remain defiantly silent but must have reconsidered because he finally croaked, 'Gold.'

'Who's behind all this?'

The wounded man struggled for breath and then seemed to spit out a name, 'Cr-ooked Foot.'

Then, as though the effort had been too much, he choked, stared wildly at Jim and the life light went from his eyes.

Seeking a clue to the man's identity, Jim quickly searched his corpse. A buckskin pouch on his belt yielded a smaller, heavy pouch containing something hard and lumpy. He had a fair idea of the bag's contents as he slipped it into his pocket but had no chance to examine it.

He could hear horses approaching and wasted no time in hurrying back to his mount and catching the reins.

'They're comin' back,' Barney said urgently.

As if to emphasize the warning, a bullet struck the dirt within inches of Jim. Jamming the dead man's revolver in his belt, he quickly arranged his reins as he prepared to mount.

Barney glimpsed a target and sent a rifle shot back at their enemies but had no way of knowing the result. He had already put away his Winchester and was wheeling his horse to flee as Jim vaulted into the saddle. Bullets were buzzing past them like angry bees as they spurred their horses around a sheltering bend in the trail. Once out of sight, they slowed to a steady trot to save their mounts as much as possible. Frequent backward glances confirmed that they were not being followed and both guessed that the attackers had only advanced far enough to collect their dead.

Another mile and another bend in the trail found them staring at the carcase of the grey horse that had been carrying Rowley's two men.

Barney pointed to a blood-stained patch on the animal's flank. 'That horse must have been carryin' lead when it passed us. Those two *hombres* are lucky they got this far.'

The tracks of two men showed plainly on the road and one seemed to be supporting the other. Jim and Barney had limited vision as they sought the missing men because the trail had many bends as it wound around the lower slopes of a mountain range.

'I reckon they heard us coming and took to the brush,' Jim said. 'They never saw us so might not know that we are friendly. Let's hope they aren't waiting in ambush for us somewhere along the trail.'

They need not have worried because they found the two men around the next bend in the trail. They were not alone.

Doc Brophy's wagon was halted.

Angela was holding the reins while her husband and one of the fugitives helped an obviously wounded man into the back. Cassius watched them suspiciously as they approached.

'Them Brophys must be crazy comin' out here with no protection at a time like this,' Barney muttered.

'They have protection,' Jim replied. 'Look in the brush on your side of the trail.'

Zeke was sitting there on his pony with a repeating rifle cradled in his arms and a grim look in his eyes. 'Howdy, boys,' he greeted. 'What's been happenin'?'

'We had a dust-up with the ones that ambushed Rowley's bunch,' Barney told him. 'We killed two — an Indian and a white man — then we got the hell out of the place. They followed us for a bit but I think they've given up the chase.'

Jim added, 'We don't know what happened to Rowley's bunch. We never got that far down the trail.'

The former scout looked concerned. 'Do you know the name of the white man you shot?'

Jim shook his head. 'He died pretty soon after I got to him and he had nothing on him that told us who he was. He was a big, dark-haired, sonofabitch with a beard and wearing buckskins — looked like a hunter or a scout. I reckon you might have known him but Barney and I are strangers around here.'

'Did he say why they attacked Rowley?'

'He couldn't say much but seemed to be blaming things on an Indian with a name that sounded like Crooked Foot. Do you know him?'

Zeke looked surprised. He turned around to ensure that he was not overheard by the people at the wagon and paused a while as though considering how much information he should divulge. Then he said quietly, 'Crooked Foot has been behind a lot of trouble around here. He was a Sioux war chief.

We don't know a lot about him but there's a legend that he can't be killed. We heard from friendly Indians that he had been killed about a year ago in a fight with the Pawnees. Now some are saying that he was only wounded and has been hiding out but if he's back on the scene, a lot of young hot-heads will follow him. Don't breathe a word about him because news gets around and peaceful Indians that hang around towns still talk to their wild cousins. He could be the leader that a whole heap of hostiles are lookin' for. With the right leader they can play hell around here. Tell no one about Crooked Foot, not even Doc Brophy. I'll get word to the army that he's back on the scene.'

'I thought you were done with the army,' Barney reminded.

'I am, but this is serious. If Crooked Foot is back they have to expect big trouble. You can talk about the fight you just had but whatever you do, don't mention Crooked Foot. I'll quietly tell the army but we can't afford dangerous rumours that he has returned from the grave.'

'That dying renegade also mentioned gold. He seemed to think that was behind the attacks they were making.'

'That figures,' Zeke said knowingly. 'If there was no gold here the white men would not be flooding in. The Black Hills were safe Indian land until such time as gold was found. The Indians will lose, they always do, but a lot of blood will be spilt before all this trouble blows over. Now let's head back to town. Tonight I'll creep out again and look up some old Indian friends of mine. They might have heard something about Crooked Foot.'

The three men rode back to where Angela was skilfully turning the wagon on the narrow trail. They watched as she worked the mules around in a very confined space until they were pointed back toward town.

'That was a real neat piece of drivin',' Barney observed, 'and she did it without a single cuss word. I'll bet she says 'please' and 'thank you' to those mules.'

'How are your patients?' Jim called as he came abreast of the wagon.

'One is fine but my husband is a bit worried about Mr Kienzle. He has a bullet in his chest. The sooner we get him back to White Rock, the better. They were lucky to escape. They were lagging behind the others and were not too deeply into the ambush when the shooting started.'

'You shouldn't be out here, Mrs Brophy,' Barney said seriously. 'It ain't safe.'

She laughed. 'We needed a driver and these mules work best for me. With Zeke and Cassius to guard us and a rifle under the wagon seat, I felt pretty safe. We knew too that you and Mr Stinson were somewhere out ahead of us.'

'It might be fine to know where we were but knowin' where the bad ones are is the tricky part,' Barney told her.

8

That evening Jim played a hunch and took the dead renegade's revolver when he went for his evening meal at Buffalo's. It was a well-worn Remington .44 converted from percussion to take .44 Henry rifle cartridges. Four notches were carved in the wooden butt. 'I was wondering,' he said, 'if you have seen any of your customers with a gun like this.'

Recognition dawned immediately. 'Sure have,' Buffalo said. 'I actually took this gun off a drunk who was causing trouble in here one night. He was a big fella, named Pete Gordon. He was mighty proud of those notches, reckoned they were four men he killed in gunfights. I gave the gun back to him when he was sober again.'

'What did Gordon do for a living?'

'I think he worked a spell for the

army as a scout or a mule-packer, something like that. The army only takes big men as packers on account of the loads they have to lift onto the mules. Ask Zeke about him — they worked together at some stage. All those buckskin characters knew each other. How did you get his gun?'

'He got shot today. He was one of the party that ambushed Rowley's men this morning. He won't be carving any more notches.' Then, as an afterthought Jim asked, 'Is Henry Rhodes still working for you?'

'Sure is. He's a good worker. He's in the back room peeling spuds at present. Just go through that door there and you'll find him.'

Jim found Henry just finishing the last of a pile of potatoes. The boy looked up in surprise.

'I have a gun for you,' Jim announced and displayed the big Remington. 'A man needs a gun around here. This one's a bit old but it's in good condition. I figured you might be able to use it.'

'I sure need a gun, or I reckon I might, one day. Thanks, Jim. Where did you get it?'

'I got it off a white renegade who happened to collide with a bullet today. I think he was connected to the attack on the survey camp. Seeing as you lost all your belongings I thought you might like to get a few things together again. This gun has been converted from cap-and-ball and will take .44 Henry cartridges. Now, be careful, there are five cartridges in that gun so don't shoot yourself or anyone else that don't need shooting.'

'I'm used to guns,' Henry said. 'We had them back home in Kansas. If I'd had one when the camp was attacked things might have been different.'

'They sure would have been: you'd be dead.'

The boy frowned and shook his head. 'I should be dead. It was only luck that I was not seen.'

'I agree with you. I've seen that creek bank you hid behind and I don't know how those redskins missed seeing you.'

After leaving the eatery Jim called to check on the wounded man they had brought in. He did not see the patient who was resting but Doc was a little more confident of his survival. He had managed to extract the bullet, which had not done as much damage as was first feared.

Inquiries revealed that Zeke had not returned to town. According to Murphy at the bar, the scout was sometimes absent for several days when he was seeking information from unnamed, old acquaintances.

Jim was on his way back to meet Barney and check on the horses when he remembered the buckskin pouch he had taken from Gordon's body. Untying the drawstring he reached into it and his fingers encountered what at first felt like small stones but when he drew one out the dull gleam revealed that he was holding a gold nugget. The weight of the pouch told him that it contained the equivalent of a large sum of money. Very quickly he returned the gold to his pocket.

Barney was playing checkers with Dawson when he returned to their camp. The former was not coping well with the idleness that the siege of the town had forced upon him. He had been away from home for too long. Even returning as a failure seemed preferable to remaining any longer in White Rock. The fact that he was losing every game to Dawson only increased his frustration. With a few deft moves the corral owner put the cowboy out of his misery and the checker playing finished.

'You're lucky we ain't playing for money,' Dawson chuckled as he picked up the board and checkers and retreated to his cabin.

Later the pair took stock of their finances. It was not a large task as they were both almost broke. They had lived frugally during their hunt for Mason and had added to their funds by taking a little short-term work but the trail back to their homes in Texas would be a long one that also promised to be a hungry one.

'Unless we can pick up a bit of work on the way back,' Barney said gloomily, 'we'll die of starvation before we get back to Texas.'

Jim produced the poke of gold from his pocket. 'Things ain't quite that bad. I took this off Gordon. It's full of gold nuggets. I don't know what it's worth but there should be enough to get us home. If there's any left over we can split it among the four families that Mason swindled but I doubt there would be anywhere near enough to make good their losses.'

Barney asked to see the gold and weighed the pouch in his hand. 'I wonder who Gordon stole this from. It seems to be all nuggets.'

'So what's unusual about that?'

'From what I understand nuggets like this are on the surface or in creek gravel and are easy to find. I think Gordon or whoever he took it from must have

99

struck gold somewhere.'

'Maybe he just robbed a lucky prospector. But let's keep our mouths shut about this. There's no point in starting a stampede when we have no idea where this gold came from. Remember — we tell no one.'

'There's one problem about this gold, Jim. How do we turn it into cash around here?'

'We don't. We wait till we get to a proper town with a bank where they trade in gold. Then we can turn it into greenbacks and maybe send some of it home. There are some strange things going on around here and I have a funny feeling that the less we pretend to know about gold, the safer we are.'

'I think you're worryin' too much,' Barney said, 'but it won't hurt us to be careful.'

★   ★   ★

Mindful of the attempted horse raid, the two cowboys rolled out their bedrolls close to Dawson's corrals and slept with their guns handy.

Jim was not sure how long he had been asleep when the dog's deep-throated bark awakened him. He was a good hundred yards from where the Brophys had set up their tent but through the still night air he heard Angela say sharply, 'Be quiet, Cassius.'

There was plenty around a small town to disturb a dog: stray cats, raccoons or even venturesome coyotes regularly upset town dogs. But Cassius had gone quiet and the cowboy surrendered to sleep once more.

He was not sure how long he had been asleep when the barking started anew. This time Doc Brophy's voice sharply reprimanded the dog but then Jim heard Angela say, 'There's something about, Nelson. Cassius never barks for the sake of it.'

Jim was beginning to think the same thing. He remembered the well-trained dogs on his parents' ranch. If they barked, there was a reason for it.

Quietly he put aside his blankets and pulled on his boots. He took his gunbelt but crawled to the deep shadows near the corral before he stood up and buckled it into place.

Barney woke up briefly. 'I hope you're goin' to shoot that damn dog,' he mumbled.

'I'm just going for a look about. Don't sleep too soundly.'

'If anyone chases you, don't come this way. I need my sleep.'

The moon was waning and visibility was poor. Try as he might, Jim could see nothing unusual but then Cassius started barking again. Once more his owners' hushed voices carried through the night as they discussed the disturbance their dog was making.

The horses were dozing in the corrals and Jim was beginning to think that Barney had been right to stay in his blankets. It was cold and he wished he had thought to put on a coat. But already it was too late. A faint sound came to his ears and looking toward its origin, he thought he saw a furtive movement under a stand of trees about thirty paces away. He looked hard again and saw nothing but some instinct warned him to stay where he was. While still mentally reproaching himself for being overly nervous, he saw something moving again; he was sure that it was a man.

9

The shape was just a little paler than the surrounding background but was as high as a crouching man and did not move like an animal.

Jim drew his Colt and as he cocked it, demanded, 'Who's there?'

There was a sound as though someone had stumbled against something on the ground, a muffled curse and a gunshot threw a streak of red flame in Jim's direction.

He threw himself on the ground and fired back. The gun spat flame from the darkness again but the bullet went high — hasty shots in poor light always did. Unable to see his sights, and hoping that he had corrected sufficiently for the darkness, Jim directed another bullet in the general direction of his opponent's gunflash.

Another unseen shooter opened fire

on the cowboy's right and the bullet passed close enough for him to feel its draught. He rolled frantically to one side and tried to locate his second attacker.

The shots woke Barney and he grabbed his rifle. He saw three muzzle flashes but did not know which one was from Jim's gun. 'Where are you, Jim?' he shouted.

'On your right. Be careful, there's a couple of them.'

Dawson's back door creaked open. 'Where are they?'

'There's one under the trees and another off to my right.' Just in time he remembered. 'Don't shoot that way — the Brophy tent is over there.'

The doctor bellowed back. 'We're under cover. I'm going to let the dog loose. Don't shoot him by mistake. He'll soon flush them out.'

'No, Nelson,' Angela pleaded. 'He could be killed.'

But Mrs Brophy need not have worried for it seemed that the attackers were beating a hasty retreat. No more shots were fired, running footsteps were heard and a short time later they heard the sound of galloping horses.

'Is anyone hurt?' Brophy called.

After a couple of negative replies he donned boots and a dressing gown and with a lantern in hand, went to confer with the others. Angela remained in the tent.

A small crowd of armed men in various stages of undress had gathered at Dawson's corrals. There was a babble of curious voices as each tried to determine the nature of the distur-bance. Since the day's ambush of Rowley's party the townspeople were seriously disturbed. The presence of a mixed band of renegades so close to the settlement was the main worry and it seemed that they were behind the latest disturbance. The general opinion was that intruders had made another attempt to steal the horses.

Jim and Barney had their own ideas but preferred not to voice their suspicions at the time.

'I wish Zeke was here,' Jim said. 'It would be interesting to see if our visitors left any tracks. He would soon be able to tell us a bit about those characters.'

'I can tell you somethin' already,' Barney said quietly. 'They ain't after horses. They're after us.'

'But why us?'

'Maybe they know we took that Gordon fella's gold. He might have been their banker. Or maybe they think we learned somethin' about what's really goin' on around here. Sure as hell somethin's happenin' here that we ain't supposed to know about.'

★　★　★

Zeke arrived next morning red-eyed and haggard. He steered his weary pony to Dawson's corrals where Jim and Barney were feeding their animals. 'Howdy, boys. What's been happening?'

They told him as he unsaddled and

attended to his horse. The scout asked the odd question but mostly just listened to their account of the night's excitement.

'I'd like to know what's behind the night visitors we've been having lately,' Jim told him.

Zeke looked at him, his face serious. 'I can tell you now that last night's raid was probably in revenge. You boys killed Crooked Foot yesterday and that dashed the hopes of a lot of Sioux who thought they had a new leader. I rode a lot of miles last night visitin' people it ain't safe to be seen with in daylight but the word was already around.'

Jim still had doubts. 'There are white men mixed up in this business too, and the late-lamented Mr Gordon claimed that there was also gold involved.'

Anger showed briefly on Zeke's face. 'There's always gold causin' trouble somewhere. If there was no gold in the Black Hills, the Lakota would have settled down and greedy white men would not be there tearin' the place apart. Gold's a curse and we sure didn't need it around these parts.'

Barney inquired, 'With Crooked Foot dead, do you reckon things will quieten down?'

'Don't even mention that name around here. The army's convinced he's dead but the Indians will be expectin' him to come back to life and lead them to victory if they know he has appeared back on the scene. Livin' or dead Crooked Foot is still mighty important to them. He's strong medicine.'

'What do the whites think about him?' Jim asked.

'Most have never heard of him and we need to keep it that way. There are half-breeds here in town who have relatives among the Lakota. If they as much as pick up a rumour, the word will get back to them.'

'That's what I don't understand.' Jim was puzzled. 'Surely the Sioux know that their great war chief is back.'

Zeke wiped a hand wearily across his face. 'From what I have managed to find out, Crooked Foot was hidin' out with a small group of trusted warriors. He was badly wounded and his men feared that some of the agency Indians would betray him to the army. The soldiers would have hunted him down if they could. You have to trust me on this. I know it sounds strange but there is a good reason for this secrecy. Don't mention Crooked Foot until I tell you it's safe.' He continued, 'Right now though, I'm goin' to grab some shuteye. I'm worn out.'

Jim had one more question. 'How much longer do Barney and I need to stay around here? It's time we were headed back to Texas.'

'Just hold on another couple of days. I've heard that an army patrol is headed this way and they should be able to tell you if the road is clear to the south.'

Barney was having trouble filling in his time and was keen to leave White Rock behind him. Dawson had beaten him so many times at checkers that it was embarrassing and finances did not allow long sessions in Murphy's saloon. For the want of something better to do, he was wandering aimlessly past the Brophy's tent when Cassius strolled out, saw him and trotted across.

'Howdy, you old hound,' he said. The dog came up to him with its tongue lolling out of its mouth and its tail wagging. Barney stopped and patted the animal's head. 'You didn't do a bad job last night for a walkin' flea farm.'

'Cassius does not have fleas,' Angela announced in a severe voice as she appeared from around the side of their wagon. Though secretly amused, she pretended to frown. 'Last night he saved us all from being murdered in our beds. He's a hero.'

'Maybe he is,' Barney admitted, 'but he gives a good imitation of a dog — a good dog though.'

Angela laughed. 'You are being very diplomatic this morning, Mr Olsen.'

'My name's Barney. When folks call me mister I start lookin' around to see if my old man's about. It's the same with Jim. You don't need to be so formal. After all we shared the same gunfight last night.'

'In that case, Barney, call me Angela. Comrades in arms must not be too formal.'

In his attempt to find something to say, Barney asked, 'How is your painting going?'

'I haven't done a lot lately but would you like to see some of my sketches?'

The cowboy had nothing better to do. 'Sure would.'

Reaching into the back of the wagon, Angela produced a large folder containing several pencil sketches on cartridge paper. 'These are a few I did at Fort Abraham Lincoln.' She passed over a large drawing of an Indian's head. 'This was one of the army scouts.'

Barney was very impressed by the likeness. The solemn face staring from the page was unmistakably drawn from life. It was the Indian's hairstyle that caught his eye. The hair was roached up in front like the Indian they had recently shot. 'That's a good picture. Is that fella a Sioux?'

'Hardly. His name is Walking Dog and he's a Crow scout working for the army. The Crows and the Sioux don't like each other. That hairstyle is a sure sign of the Crow tribe.'

'I ain't too familiar with these northern tribes but I thought the Sioux might have done their hair like that too.'

Angela shook her head. 'I don't think so. There is a lot of bad blood between the two tribes. The Crows are friendly to our people but I was told that they and the Sioux had been traditional enemies before the white men came.'

Together the pair looked at a few more drawings. There were many good likenesses of frontier types, soldiers, Indians, horses and other animals and Barney enjoyed seeing them but the picture of the Crow scout intrigued him. Then suddenly he knew why.

As politely as he could he took his leave of the doctor's wife and hurried back to Dawson's corrals where he knew that he would find Jim.

The latter was seated in the shade on a canvas pack cover cleaning his gun. He looked up as his partner approached. 'You look like you have something important on your mind, Barney.'

'You're dead right. I think someone has been lyin' to us.'

10

Jim did not seem shocked by his friend's announcement. 'That don't surprise me any. Which particular lie has got you so upset?'

'The story that we killed Crooked Foot yesterday. The fella we shot was a Crow, not a Sioux.'

That revelation certainly caught Jim's attention. 'How do you know?'

'Angela Brophy told me that only Crows do their hair like that dead Indian's. I saw the same hairdo on one of her drawings.'

Jim frowned. 'Would she know? She ain't even American.'

'She's been in this neck of the woods for a couple of years and has seen more of these northern tribes than we have. I reckon she'd know.'

Still unconvinced, Jim asked, 'But why would Zeke tell us that Crooked

Foot was a Sioux and that he was dead?'

'Could be he was given the wrong story.'

'But why?'

'He probably didn't see the dead fella and could be relyin' on word from someone else. That's one reason I can think of straight away.'

'I just had another idea,' Jim said. 'What if this Crooked Foot character isn't an Indian at all? We've both met men on the frontier who have strange nicknames.'

Barney pretended concern. 'Just settle down, Jim. You've had two ideas in quick succession. Don't strain your brain. Why in tarnation would a white man be leadin' Indians against other white men?'

'Gordon told us as he was dying that gold was behind all this. Suppose this Crooked Foot was really after gold and was killing folks and blaming it on the Sioux and Cheyenne.'

'That's possible,' Barney admitted.

'But why would this coyote be after us?'

'Because we know about the gold and we've been to Antler Creek. Most of the others who went there were killed.'

'I'm glad you mentioned that. The most obvious character to be named Crooked Foot is Rowley but he's dead.'

'How do we know? Suppose he led the others into a trap that he set himself. Think back on the day we went to Antler Creek. We could have been killed that day if Zeke hadn't kept such a good lookout. I reckon that you and I are marked down for killing because someone thinks we know more than we do. Being in White Rock don't seem too healthy to me any more. Instead of hanging around here waiting to be killed, we should be out looking for a few answers.'

'Ain't you forgettin' there's war parties watchin' the roads? Zeke says we should wait till the army tells us the roads are safe.'

Jim thought deeply before replying. 'If those war parties are as dangerous as

Zeke says, we should have seen more signs of them being around. There's been no smoke from burning houses or people coming into town from abandoned homesteads. You and I saw all those things in Texas when the Comanches were on the prod.'

'You could be right. I was talkin' to a couple of miners who came up the trail yesterday. But they had been warned that things between here and the Black Hills can be pretty dangerous. They're gonna stay here until the army clears the trail.'

'How do you feel about a ride up to Antler Creek?' Jim was reassembling his Colt as he spoke. Then he added, 'A ride that no one knows about, just the two of us.'

'What's behind all this?'

As he placed cartridges in the gun's cylinder, Jim said, 'If we find where Rowley and the others were ambushed, we should find his body if he is not Crooked Foot. Then I reckon we could go up along Antler Creek for a while and see what's there that is getting men killed.'

Barney was every bit as curious as his partner but suddenly remembered why they were in the area. Even as a bearer of bad news, he knew that they had a responsibility to people in Texas. 'I dunno ... What are we likely to find? Will it serve any real purpose?'

'There's a good chance we can find out why folks are trying to kill us and maybe remove any threats at the same time. Let's carry the fight to the enemy.'

'That would be a mighty fine idea if we knew who the enemy was.'

'I reckon we'll find out when we have a bit of a look around.'

'What if the enemy finds us first?'

'Do you really think someone is going to watch the road twenty-four hours a day? The Indians know the times when most folks travel; they won't be watching the trail at a time when no one in his right mind would be using it. We can slip out of town in the dark and be most of the way to Antler Creek before daylight. If anyone is around chances are that they won't be expecting to see us and we'll see them first.'

Barney gave a wry smile. 'If I didn't know it was being proposed by a crazy man, I'd think it might work.'

'So you'll go with me?'

'It beats gettin' whipped at checkers by Dawson. That man would turn even a nice fella like me into a bad loser.'

They spent the rest of the afternoon quietly preparing for their journey. Both horses received extra feeds and the men put together some basic rations to sustain them for a day. The nights were still cold and they stored the food and spare rifle ammunition in the large pockets of their blanket-lined canvas coats. Saddle-bags were not considered; the ride would be a long one and the riders were loath to burden their horses with any unnecessary weight.

That evening they ate well at Buffalo's place and even risked complimentary cups of coffee as they padded out their meal with extra slices of home-baked bread. They were not sure when, if ever, they would have another decent meal.

11

Only Cassius heard them leave. He gave one warning bark.

'Be quiet, you old flea farm,' Barney called back softly.

Whether in response to the order or the feeling that he had done his duty, the dog fell silent.

Neither rider spoke again until they were well clear of White Rock. The night was moonless and in the dark landscape the horses were left to find the trail. They would keep to where the going was easiest.

'I don't think the Sioux would be wasting sleeping time guarding this trail tonight,' Jim said. 'Not too many folks would travel at this hour.'

'Not too many sane ones anyway,' Barney growled as he turned up his coat collar against the night chill.

Somewhere in the distance a wolf

howled, an eerie sound that did nothing to ease the anxiety of the two riders. They rode with all senses alert even though they were fairly confident that no ambush was waiting for them. The trail to Antler Creek was reasonably well defined in daylight but on a pitch black night it could be missed. People often overestimated travel distances at night where progress was slower and as neither possessed a watch it was difficult to know exactly how long they had been travelling. Cloud prevented any guidance from the stars.

They kept conversation to a minimum for safety's sake but finally the pair halted and compared calculations. Both agreed that they had to be close to the branch in the trail.

'I seem to remember that there was a little trickle of water not far from the fork,' Jim said quietly. 'I don't think we have crossed that yet.'

Barney had a few doubts though. 'Them little trickles can dry out in a matter of hours sometimes and that one was narrow enough for a horse to step across and we wouldn't notice it.'

'I know that but we would be dead unlucky for both horses to walk across without one putting afoot in it and making a splash. I'm pretty sure we haven't passed it yet.'

Jim's optimism was well founded because a couple of minutes later they heard the reassuring splash as the horses stepped gingerly through the tiny stream. They found the turn off to Antler Greek a short distance further on and then could relax a little. At least they were headed in the right direction. But as the danger of missing the trail was gone the new one of a possible ambush had now increased.

With such poor visibility, danger would be almost impossible to see so the two cowboys relied on their hearing. The movement of night animals and birds caused many a nervous intake of breath but another few miles were negotiated without incident. They were just starting to relax when the horses began to snort nervously and the riders heard faint movements ahead. Then they heard a growl and a small yip.

'Coyotes,' Jim said in relief.

'But what are they feedin' on?'

The scavengers slunk away as the men came closer and in the gloom they could just discern a dark lump on the ground. Closer inspection revealed a dead horse. It's head was pointed toward White Rock.

Jim wondered aloud how far they were from the ambush site for they had passed the survivor's dead horse half an hour before.

'It's hard to know,' Barney said softly as he looked about. 'Sometimes it takes a lot of lead to bring down a horse — depends on where it's hit.'

Both agreed that little would be gained by examining the half-eaten carcass so they did not delay.

A few minutes later they reached the scene of the ambush. The scavenger animals had started their grim work but there were two more dead horses only a few yards apart and a dead man nearby.

They dismounted and, steeling himself for what he knew he would see, Jim struck a match. The corpse was not a pretty sight but the pair recognized one of Rowley's party by the distinctive plaid jacket he had been wearing when they last saw him. A little further along the trail they found two more bodies but could not find Rowley or the other man of his party.

Jim peered about him. 'It makes sense that if they survived the ambush, they probably took to the brush. We won't find them in the dark so let's not waste too much time.'

'I wonder if Rowley is Crooked Foot and led the others into a trap.' Barney mounted his horse as he spoke.

'This business with Crooked Foot has really messed things up. Zeke got the story wrong if he thinks we killed him and Rowley didn't look like a Sioux war chief to me.'

'Could these *hombres* have been

murdered by some renegade Crows? If Angela Brophy's right, that fella we got was a Crow. If anyone knows the difference between a Sioux and a Crow, it should be Zeke. But is it really important? I can't see where it matters what tribe this Crooked Foot fella was as long as he's well and truly dead. Tryin' to figure out what in the hell's goin' on is strainin' my brain somethin' awful.'

Jim frowned and shook his head. 'I'm not sure what part Crooked Foot has had in all this. Suppose he didn't really exist. We only have Zeke's word about him and he's been acting mighty mysterious.'

'Don't forget that Gordon mentioned him when he was cashin' in his chips.'

'He might have been out of his head or he might have said that just to cause trouble. His voice and breathing were very feeble. Maybe we didn't hear him right. I don't think we'll find any answers around here. Let's head for Antler Creek and see what else we can find out.'

A red streak on the eastern horizon showed that dawn was approaching as the riders descended into the valley of Antler Creek. They allowed their horses to drink and then followed the stream up to the wreckage of the survey camp.

There was enough light to show that little had changed since their last visit and a couple of rabbits feeding on the short grass gave notice as they fled that no other humans were around.

With slackened cinches and bitless mouths, the horses were allowed to graze about while the men ate the food they had brought with them. It was fully light when they prepared to continue their journey.

Both had removed their heavy coats and were fastening them behind their saddles when Barney glanced up along the course of the creek. He swore and pointed. 'We ain't alone here.'

Behind a distant, dark-green barrier of lodgepole pines, a faint column of smoke was rising. 'Looks like a campfire,' Jim said.

'I know that. But whose is it? I don't recall us havin' a lot of friends around here.'

Then suddenly the smoke was gone. Both men knew why. Indians, outlaws and those who feared discovery, would always extinguish campfires before it became light enough for others to see the smoke. Men with no reason to hide took no such precautions.

Barney looked at Jim. 'It looks like someone in that camp was a bit slow to put out their fire. What do you think?'

'It might only be prospectors trying not to attract trouble with the Sioux but I reckon we should just creep up there and have a look around. It could be Gordon's friends and I can't see them welcoming us with open arms.'

They moved forward carefully, staying under cover where they could and pausing to survey the scene ahead when they had to cross open ground. A ride that normally would have taken only a few minutes, took nearly half an hour but neither man begrudged the extra time. It was better than riding into an ambush.

At one stage they travelled along the edge of the creek bank at a point where the water was wider and shallow. Barney pointed at the gravel on the water's edge. 'Someone's been diggin' here. Look how the gravel has all been turned over.'

'Do you think it might have been Andrews and his surveyors?'

'I doubt it. As far as is known, they didn't get this far along the creek. More likely it's a prospector.'

'It certainly wasn't Sioux or Cheyenne. A war party wouldn't be scratching around but white renegades might. Gordon got that gold from somewhere. It wouldn't be the first time someone's been killed to conceal a new gold strike.'

Barney did not agree. 'It's only a matter of time before some prospector comes up this way and if there is gold here, the secret won't be safe for long. They can't kill everybody.'

'That's true. But it could be that

there's people here picking up the easy stuff before the rush starts — folks that normally would not be full-time miners.'

'But they would still stake claims. Let's keep movin' and chances are that we'll find a bunch of prospectors already at work with claims pegged out.'

'You're probably right, but let's go mighty carefully.'

*   *   *

Jerry Fitch was out early. The camp needed fresh meat and the little man knew a grassy flat along the creek where deer often grazed in the early morning. He was an excellent hunter moving silently along the ridge where he could look into the creek valley without going too close. From an elevated position he could see any deer without the risk of a stray gust of wind betraying him.

Something was moving in the brush near the creek's edge; he caught a splash of colour, something blue, like a shirt. Then the distinctive coat of an Appaloosa showed in a thinner patch of trees.

Fitch sank to his knees behind a sheltering boulder. It was unlikely that anyone would see him but he was not one to take chances. Peering around the edge of the rock, he could see the tiny figures of two horsemen halted at the edge of the creek. The bank was high at that point so there was no place to water horses. He saw them standing in their stirrups and the one in the blue shirt on the dark brown horse was pointing down.

Fitch knew what had caught their attention. He had tried a bit of gold panning at that particular place. They were looking at the results of his unsuccessful efforts. Though he was too far away to identify the riders, the little man knew he had seen that Appaloosa before.

If the strangers followed the creek they could be ten minutes from the camp. Fitch could take a shorter cut over the ridge but he was on foot and would have to hurry if he was to warn the others in the camp. Though on the wrong side of forty, he was still a very fit man. Silently cursing the intruders, he rose to his feet and set out jog-trotting toward the camp. He knew he would get there before the two riders but they needed to lay plans for a successful ambush. These men had already killed two of his companions and Fitch was determined that this time they would not escape. Crooked Foot had already decided that the pair were the greatest threat to their operations. The attempt on their lives at Dawson's corrals had failed but this time there would be no barking dogs.

12

Fitch was panting heavily when he came down the ridge to the camp. Even as camps go, it was very basic — just supplies and saddles piled under a tarpaulin, a temporary corral with horses and mules, a fireplace and a few scattered bedrolls. 'Two riders' — he gasped — 'comin' along the creek.'

Idaho dropped the makings of the cigarette he was rolling and ran to grab the rifle leaning against a nearby tree. Sol Paulson, a wiry little half-breed, heard the message and ran to where his two Crow cousins, Bent Arrow and Tall Beaver were making temporary repairs to a broken corral rail. A few rapid words in the Crow language diverted them from their task and sent them running for their weapons.

'They should be round the end of that ridge any minute,' Fitch said.

'They're followin' the creek. We'll get good clear shots so nobody fire too soon. Let 'em get out in the open. Don't shoot till they see the camp.' The five men looked about and each sought a position where they would have a clear view of the open ground on the creek flat.

'The country's openin' out,' Barney said. 'If we follow the creek we'll be out in the open when we come round the end of that ridge. We'd be sittin' shots for anyone who was waitin' behind that hill and that's roughly where that camp would be.'

Jim agreed. 'I was thinking the same thing. It might be safer if we stay in the trees and cross over the ridge. We must be pretty close to that camp by now.

They turned their horses away from the creek and set them at the rocky tree-covered ridge that ran at right angles to it. Moving up the steep incline was noisy and in places the horses dislodged loose rocks that rolled back down the slope, but little could be done about that. It was still safer in the trees than riding out in the open.

Eventually they reached the crest of the hill and saw a large grassy flat running from the creek bank back into the trees in a small U-shaped valley. Both riders halted and surveyed the scene while the horses recovered from the steep climb.

'There's something over there,' Jim said quietly and pointed across the valley.

Barney leaned forward in the saddle and looked in the direction indicated. He could view the scene from a slightly different angle. 'It's horses in a corral. There's a few of 'em. I wonder where their riders are.'

'Let's get off the skyline first and then we'll try to find out. With claim jumpers and Indians about, we'd better be careful — some of these prospectors are more than a bit trigger-happy. It's safest that we see them before they see us.'

Cautiously the pair started to descend

the slope weaving their mounts around trees and other obstructions as they went on separate courses. Halfway down the hill they came together again,

'There's some sort of camp down there,' Barney said in a low voice, 'but where is everyone? If their horses are here, why ain't they?'

'Because they're laying up somewhere waiting to ambush us. Let's get over there among those rocks and see if we can see what's going on.'

As quietly as they could, the two rode across to the clump of boulders they had selected. They were almost there when the horses in the corral caught their scent and one whinnied. Almost immediately Barney's horse whinnied back.

'Damn blabbermouth,' Barney said as he slipped from the saddle and drew his carbine.

Jim wasted no time imitating him and it was just as well because Bent Arrow had noted the origin of the sound, wheeled about and snapped a shot from his Sharps carbine. 'Up hill!' he called to the others.

'They're behind us,' Fitch yelled as he moved to the opposite side of the large pine that had concealed him.

Paulson looked behind to see the two led horses disappearing among the boulders. He did not waste a shot and instead looked about for better protection. The little ridge of rock had been ample while shooting downhill but was not much use against opponents above him. He dived behind an old, mossy log and hoped that the wood was still strong enough to stop a rifle bullet.

Bent Arrow slipped quietly into a nearby patch of undergrowth. He was sure that he had not been seen and had no intention of changing that situation. The others could keep the intruders busy. He would fight them his way.

Paulson peered over his log and withdrew his face in alarm as a bullet tore away a large piece of rotten wood and missed him by inches.

Idaho had found reasonable cover

and threw a quick shot in Jim's direction, missing his target and betraying his position.

'How many are there?' Barney called.

'I count three — one behind that old log, another a few yards to his left behind a big tree and there's powder smoke hanging over a clump of bushes about fifty yards away on my right front.'

'You'd better make that four.' Barney had seen Tall Beaver darting between trees as he sought to flank their position. 'One of them's an Injun. He's tryin' to work round us.'

'Keep an eye on him. I'll try to keep the others busy.'

The bullets were whining off the rocks above the cowboys' heads as their opponents fired ranging shots. Firing uphill had them at a slight disadvantage but the renegades could keep up a steady stream of lead that kept their opponents undercover.

By this time Bent Arrow had moved far to the right of his companions and now started to ascend the ridge. He moved slowly and carefully and had no intention of drawing fire upon himself while behind such flimsy cover as a few bushes. Without having seen him, he knew that his fellow Crow would be making similar moves but the intensity of the defenders' gunfire from the other side indicated that he might have been detected.

Jim peered through a narrow crack between two boulders. It was too small to push his rifle barrel through but gave him a reasonable view of the ground to the front. He was looking at the log when he saw just the faintest sign of movement. Sunlight had momentarily flashed on the muzzle of a rifle before the man holding it pulled it back under cover. The weapon had appeared just behind a conspicuous knot on the log so the cowboy used it to mark the rifleman's location. He found a sheltered spot in weeds at the base of a boulder. The field of fire was limited but he did have a good view of the log and was well concealed. Lining his sights on the upper edge of the fallen timber, he waited. It was a gamble because he was not watching their other enemies and could only hope that they were on the defensive.

There was movement and Jim squeezed the trigger without taking time to identify his target. When the powder smoke cleared, he saw a long splinter missing from the top edge of the log. He was reasonably sure that he had not missed but it had all happened in the blinking of an eye.

He should not have worried though because Paulson was flat on his back as the result of a bullet passing front to back through his skull. He would never have known what hit him.

Any speculation about his last shot ended quickly when a bullet hit the boulder about two feet above Jim's head and the ricochet almost hit him as it buried itself in the ground. This was his first indication that Bent Arrow was on their flank and above him. He quickly rolled to a more sheltered position.

'There's another one on my side,' he called to Barney.

'You should've been watchin' for somethin' like that. They must have us just about surrounded now.'

Jim ignored his friend's criticism. He had more important matters on his mind. Another of Bent Arrow's bullets showered him with little specks of stone before it whined off into the distance after hitting the boulder. There was every chance that a misshapen lump of lead would find its target after bouncing off a rock. 'I have to change position,' he called to Barney. 'Keep an eye out for those downhill for me.'

'Do it quick — and try not to get yourself shot.'

Jim rose to a half crouch and as quickly as he could, sprinted to a larger rock. A bullet smashed against it as he threw himself under cover again.

The new position gave him a different outlook up the hill behind them. His eye detected movement on the opposite side to where Bent Arrow was firing. Someone in buckskins, his hair in long plaits was belly down, wriggling into a position that would give him a clear shot at Barney. Even as Jim watched he saw the prone Indian raising a Henry rifle.

Throwing caution to the wind, Jim stood up and lined his sights on the rifleman. The movement caught the Indian's eye. He gave one startled glance and rolled sideways to defend himself against the unexpected attack. He was fatally slow.

Jim's first bullet smashed into his shoulder and rolled him onto his back. But the man retained his hold on his rifle. Taking no chances, the cowboy sent another bullet into his target. This time the Henry repeater fell to the ground and its owner seemed no longer interested in it. He writhed violently as though in great pain and then fell back limply.

'I got another one,' Jim called. 'The

one you couldn't hit,' he added.

'I left him for you — you need the practice.'

Any other comments that Barney might have made were drowned out in a burst of gunfire as the renegades renewed their attack

Leaving his partner to handle the two riflemen downhill from them, Jim switched his aim to Bent Arrow who had been trying to work around their position. His move proved to be a timely one. The Crow suddenly found himself at a disadvantage in an area where there was little cover. With rifle bullets whizzing around him, the Indian, who had probably seen his fellow warrior's fate, turned and sprinted back down the hill. He was almost to a patch of good cover when Barney's Winchester spoke: and he tumbled end over end down the slope.

'Got the — ' Barney's triumphant shout was cut short by a bullet.

13

Zeke rode hard. It was a casual remark by Angela Brophy about the two cowboys leaving town before daylight that alerted him to their absence. When he saw that their pack mule was still at Dawson's, the former scout had no doubts about where they were going. He saddled a horse and took another as a spare.

Once clear of town he urged his mount into a gallop. Despite its nondescript appearance the bay pony was a good one. With neck outstretched and its belly low to the ground, it was soon flinging the miles behind it. One after another the familiar landmarks along the trail flashed past.

The sun was high, the heat increasing and the pony's neck and shoulders were soon coated with white foamy sweat. Foam was flying from its bit and more was forming on the animal's hindquarters. The rider made little effort to spare his mount.

They were more than halfway to their objective before Zeke felt it necessary to change ponies. He halted, transferring his saddle and bridle to his favourite roan pony that he had taken in battle from a Pawnee warrior a couple of years before.

He turned loose the weary bay. It would probably make its way home but would be no great loss if it did not — similar horses were cheap and plentiful. The roan pony seemed to sense its master's urgency and was keen to go. Zeke sat still and held it to a steady pace; time was precious and already he feared that he might be too late. The hardest part was resisting the urge to hurry his mount but he knew it was necessary. If the horse gave out before reaching Antler Creek the consequences could be disastrous.

★ ★ ★

'How bad are you hurt?'

'My right arm's hit but I don't know how badly.' Barney gasped and then added. 'It hurts to move my fingers.'

'Barney, you sure picked a bad time to get yourself shot.'

'Sorry about that. When do you suggest is a good time?'

'I'm not quite sure but next time, wait till I tell you. I suppose you can't use a rifle.'

'I can use my six-shooter left handed. If they get close enough I might be able to hit them.'

Jim worked his way through the rocks to where Barney was seated awkwardly trying to tie his bandanna around a blood-stained forearm. He offered to help but his partner declined.

'Keep a lookout. We don't want those coyotes to creep up on us. I'll try to patch myself up.'

Neither Idaho nor Fitch had any inclination to get closer but could not retreat because of the open creek flat behind them. They had seen their three associates killed and their numbers reduced so that suddenly the sides were even. Both were relatively safe behind big trees but they had nowhere to go and the two cowboys were in a much better position. To make matters worse for them, both were cut off from their horses. They did not know however, that Barney was wounded.

Gradually the shooting stopped and a stalemate developed.

Jim had found a sheltered spot from where he could view the space between them and their enemies. It was too narrow to put a gun barrel through but he could discern where their opponents were sheltering. 'We've cut down the odds,' he whispered to Barney. 'They can't come out from behind those trees. I'll just move around these rocks a bit and find a place where I can get a shot at anyone who shows himself.'

'That's fine, but I reckon we're in the same fix. If we leave these rocks they can get clear shots at us and remember they now have two rifles to our one. I can't use this arm of mine.'

'Is it bleeding much?'

'I'm not sure. It's too danged sore to bandage tightly.'

'We need to get you back to Doc Brophy. Can you ride on your own?'

'I can but I don't like the idea of runnin' from those skunks. What's your plan?'

'It's easy. You get on your horse and ride like hell to get over that ridge behind us. Our friends down there will have to show themselves to shoot at you and when they do I'll be able to get clear shots at them. Once you're over the ridge I'll make my run if I don't get them both.'

Barney had more than a few doubts. 'You can't shoot two men at once. While you're shootin' one, the other could be lettin' daylight through me.'

'There's a good chance he'll miss.'

'There's also the chance that you'll miss and I'll have two shootin' at me. Or what if I get out and you can't?'

'If you can think of a better idea, let

me hear it. But you need attention for that arm. You don't want to lose the use of it or maybe even lose the arm and it's a long ride back to White Rock.'

The wounded man thought for a while. He did not like Jim's proposal but realized that his friend was speaking sense. 'I hate to admit it but I can't think of a better idea. I'll give it a try.'

'Good. Can you mount on your own?'

'I reckon so.'

'Then get on that big elephant of yours and let me know when you are ready.'

Barney lurched to his feet and, keeping low, struggled back to the horses. Seconds later he was back. 'We ain't goin' anywhere,' he announced.

'What do you mean?'

'I mean there's a big bunch of Indians sittin' up there on that ridge we came over. They're watchin' this little disagreement.'

'Are they wearing war paint? They might just be a hunting party.'

'I couldn't see about the paint but

chances are they're huntin' us.'

Leaving Barney to keep an eye on their white adversaries, Jim worked his way through the rocks until he could see up the ridge behind their position. Sure enough, the Indians were there sitting silently on their ponies and watching the scene below. An exact count was not possible but Jim reckoned there were at least a dozen.

Then as he watched, one warrior on a buckskin pony rode out from the group. He gesticulated, pointing down into the valley and waving an arm about as though urging his companions to attack. The faint sound of an angry voice could be heard although Jim would not have understood the language even if he had been closer. The body language was that of an aggressive man urging his comrades to attack.

Jim raised his voice just loudly enough for Barney to hear. 'Looks like our fine feathered friends are keen to buy into this fight. I reckon they'll take a hand soon.'

'You sure know how to cheer a man up,' Barney replied. 'I wonder if they're in cahoots with that bunch down the hill?'

'Knowing our luck, they probably are. I'll give you my six-shooter and I'll take both rifles. Don't shoot till you have to because you won't hit anyone left-handed until they get close. We'll have to make every shot count because I'm not sure we'll get a chance to reload.'

Whatever comment Barney was about to make, was replaced instead by a gasp of surprise. Then he called to Jim, 'It's Zeke! He's just come round the end of the ridge.'

From the creek bank the scout shouted, 'Nobody shoot — I'm comin' up. Don't shoot if you want to get out alive.' Then the former scout started yelling in the Lakota language.

Jim saw the warriors on the hill stir and then start moving their restless ponies about as they talked among themselves.

With his right hand held palm forward in a sign of peace, the scout urged his weary pony toward the men in the camp. Watchers saw him leaning down from his saddle and engaging in animated conversation with the pair sheltering behind the trees. After a couple of minutes he turned his mount toward the rocks where Jim and Barney were sheltering.

'What's happening, Zeke?' Jim called.

The scout halted his pony, called something to the Indians on the ridge and rode closer. 'It's all one hell of a mess. I know these prospectors from my scoutin' days. They thought you two were claim jumpers. They know different now.'

'It cost them three men to learn,' Barney growled. 'They were waitin' to bushwhack us.'

'We'll talk about that later. Right now I have to start talkin' to the Sioux. They're gettin' mighty restless. If nobody shoots we might all get out of this with our hair. Now, stay put and don't make any wrong moves.'

Calling out again in the Lakota tongue, Zeke steered his pony up the slope to where the warriors waited.

Jim and Barney heard angry voices and saw weapons brandished as the scout rode closer to the Sioux.

'It don't sound like Zeke's too popular in some quarters,' Barney observed. 'Right now I wouldn't like to trade places with him.'

Jim said, 'Knowing his former background with the army, I can understand why some of those Sioux would not exactly trust him. I think he might need to do some fast talking to get this mess fixed. We could easily have a three-sided fight here.'

'I know there might be a better time to worry about this but I'm mighty curious about what Zeke is doin' here.'

'If we live long enough, we can always ask him later,' Jim said.

14

The two cowboys saw Zeke deep in conversation with the warriors on the hill. The discussion was obviously heated with many abrupt gestures and enough finger pointing to indicate that the Indians were far from happy with someone lower on the hill. It seemed like hours but was probably only a few minutes before the scout turned his pony back down to where Jim and Barney waited. He dismounted and said, 'I've struck a deal with Walkin' Horse who's the boss of them Sioux. If no one does anything stupid we might all get out of this alive.'

Barney asked suspiciously, 'What sort of deal?'

'The deal is that we all leave here and don't come back. We also leave the dead men's horses and weapons. I can collect a few of their personal effects to notify their families but that's all. Them prospectors have to leave behind their camp gear and supplies. They take one pony each and just what they can put in their saddle-bags. Packs and spare horses have to be left behind.'

'What do we have to leave behind?' Jim asked.

'Thanks to your old uncle Zeke, you don't have to leave nothin'. They hate prospectors and seein' as you two killed three of them, you get off free as long as you stay with me. It seems that some Sioux will still take my word. Now sit tight and don't make any rash moves. I'm goin' down to make sure them prospectors keep to the agreement. When they have left and the injuns have seen they've kept their word, us three are riding out.' He added ominously, 'If we're lucky . . . '

The pair watched Zeke lead his pony down to where their late antagonists were waiting. Cautiously the two men emerged from cover and engaged in quiet conversation while casting frequent nervous glances up the hill. A few minutes later the scout unsaddled his tired pony and turned it into the corral with the other horses. Then he took a pair of saddle-bags, slung them over his shoulder and walked back up the hill to the first of the dead Crows. He knelt briefly beside the man, searched the body but took nothing. Following the contours of the hill around, he checked the second body. This time he took a small pouch from the man's belt. He extracted a few dollar bills, held them aloft so that the Indians could see it and slipped it into the saddle-bag. The Sioux placed little value on white men's paper money. A few minutes later he searched the dead white man but the big log partly obscured him from the watchers.

Meanwhile the two survivors from the camp were hurriedly bundling a few things together and rolling them to tie behind their saddles. Then they went with Zeke to the corral to select and saddle three ponies.

'So far, so good,' Jim muttered in obvious relief.

The two prospectors wasted no time saddling and mounting. Almost as though they did not believe their luck, they were still glancing nervously up the hill as they said a final few words to Zeke.

A loud Indian voice called out as the pair rode away.

'I don't speak the language,' Barney drawled, 'but I think he's tellin' them not to come back.'

'I wonder what he'll tell us,' Jim said.

Zeke led his horse up to where the others waited. 'Let's wait a while here under cover.'

Jim looked at him sharply. 'What's wrong?'

'Maybe nothin' but some of the Sioux might have set an ambush back along the trail to White Rock. If we give that pair fifteen minutes or so we'll hear any shootin' if they run into any nasty surprises.'

'Do you reckon they'll let us hang

around?' Barney said anxiously.

'I'll buy us a bit of time.' Zeke said. 'Wait here with the horses. I intend to show our little friends around the camp and let them see all the good things the others have left them. They're sure to scalp the dead ones so if you're squeamish look away and thank the Lord, it ain't you.'

Leaving his horse with the two cowboys, the scout walked up the ridge calling to the warriors as he did so.

With some degree of hesitation, the wild riders urged their ponies down to where the scout halted near Bent Arrow's corpse. They knew that two armed and nervous men were watching them and that they might be panicked into firing. A couple of warriors dismounted and quickly took possession of the dead man's firearms and ammunition. His knife, tobacco and matches were passed up to some of the others. Then one brave seized the Crow's hair. A couple of practiced slashes with a sharp knife, a foot on the chest, a sudden jerk and the scalp was held aloft. A chorus of triumphant yells followed the deed.

Zeke pointed to where the other dead Crow lay. Less suspicious of Jim and Barney by then, a group of riders went across and repeated the previous bloody exercise.

'They shouldn't be celebratin',' Barney growled. 'We shot them.'

'You should know by now that a scalp's a scalp to an Indian. It ain't as if we really wanted to collect them.'

The two white men in the rocks seemed to have been forgotten as Zeke led them to Paulson's body. Another scalp was waved aloft and then the warriors shared out the most desirable of the possessions the dead man had on his person. From there the plunderers moved to the camp and eagerly collected loot. A few were arguing already about sharing the spoils and then one reached into a pack and found a whiskey jug. It was quickly passed from one to the other.

'I don't like the look of that,' Barney frowned as he watched the scene. 'Those Injuns won't be used to the sort of rotgut in that jug. A few more drinks of that and they're likely to forget any deals they made with Zeke.'

The scout had seen the danger and was trying to divert the braves to the horses in the corral. A couple followed him but ominously, others clustered around the jug. The latter group quickly became noisier and were soon arguing in tones that grew increasingly more angry.

Zeke casually strolled away from the Indians and returned to the other white men. His voice was low but his tone was far from casual as he told them, 'It's time to go. They're gettin' likkered up and are having second thoughts about lettin' us go. Those prospectors have a long start on us now and if the Sioux have set any traps, they'll spring them first.'

'Do we run for it?' Barney asked as Jim helped him onto his horse.

'Not unless we have to. If you run, injuns will chase you. We ride out quietly and hope that nobody is takin' any real notice, but if they start shootin' or runnin' for their ponies, put your spurs to work.'

Zeke placed the saddle-bags on his horse and secured them. Then he loosened his revolver in its holster before stepping into the stirrup. 'Let's go.'

The three riders had emerged from their cover and had ridden about fifty yards before a brave saw them and shouted to them.

'Keep goin',' Zeke whispered before shouting a reply in the Lakota language.

The warrior called again and this time his tone of voice was angry.

The shouted reply from the scout did little to calm the warrior and he started pulling at the arms of his comrades and pointing up the hill at the retreating riders.

'If we can make it over the ridge,

they're likely to forget about us,' Zeke said. 'It's not far now. Don't look back or look as if you're worried.'

'That's easier said than done,' Barney muttered. 'For all we know some of them Sioux could be fixin' their sights on us already.'

It seemed an eternity before the three riders crossed the ridge. Each glanced back briefly before descending the reverse slope. To their great relief it seemed that the Sioux had already forgotten them.

Zeke took the lead once they were safely behind the ridge. 'Follow me. It's askin' for trouble to try goin' back the way we came. We're safer to go cross-country. That way we won't run into any ambushes. The Sioux told me that there were other huntin' parties out here and one of them might just be tempted to attack us if they met us along Antler Creek. It's safest if we travel through the rough country where there's not much game. It might take a bit longer but our chances of getting back to White Rock will be a hell of a lot better.'

'Is there any water where we're going?' Jim asked. 'Our horses have done a lot of travelling and they'll need a drink.'

'There's a bit of a soak about an hour's ride away. There's always water there. That will get them back to town.'

They turned across Antler Creek at a rocky crossing where their tracks would not be so obvious and the scout led them up a steep slope with the horses slipping on loose shale and panting for breath as they went up in a series of plunges until at last they climbed out of the canyon. Halting a while to allow their mounts a breather, they looked back over the scene in the valley. There was no sign of pursuit.

All agreed that their chances of getting safely back to White Rock had improved considerably.

They were on a rocky plateau sparsely timbered in places but mostly covered with sage brush. Some distance away there was a patch of forest and it was toward this that Zeke led them.

'The soak's in those trees over there,' Zeke said. 'How're you travellin', Barney?'

The wounded cowboy was far from well but did not want to show any weakness. 'I'll be better when I can get in among those shady trees. That sun sure is hot.'

'We can water the horses there and give them a rest for a while. But we can't stay too long. It's still a long ride back to town.'

It was cooler among the trees but they were not long in the shade. The trio rode a short distance into the timber and suddenly there was a clearing ahead. The midday sun was beating down on a broad grassy meadow where a faint sparkle of water showed among the grass.

Zeke turned in his saddle. 'We can take it easy for a while now.'

'I'm not so sure,' Jim said.

15

'What's the trouble?' Zeke asked.

Jim pointed to tracks showing plainly on some muddy ground about thirty yards from where they had halted. 'There's been horses through here, and not long ago.'

'Could be mustangs,' Zeke suggested.

Jim shook his head. 'I've spent a lot of time in mustang country and have seen no sign of them around here. I reckon that ridden horses made those tracks. It's either those two prospectors or possibly Indian hunters. And if it is Indians, there could be more about.'

Zeke looked puzzled. 'I doubt it would be the prospectors. They'll be heading back to White Rock by the shortest way. They wouldn't know about this place.'

'Sure as hell, someone knows about this place,' Barney growled. 'We'd be sittin' shots crossin' this open ground.'

Jim suggested, 'What if you stay here among the trees until I have a good look around?'

'It's like keepin' a dog and barkin' yourself,' Zeke protested. 'I used to get two dollars a day for doin' this but today you can have my services for free!'

'You'd be better at that work than I would,' Jim admitted.

'I've had a lot more practice. If you fellas wait here, I'll creep around through the trees and make sure there's no one waitin' to catch us as we cross that open ground. It could take an hour or so but it might be time well spent.'

Keeping within the screen of trees all three dismounted. Barney was getting weak and almost fell as he stepped down from his horse. Jim caught him by his good arm and steered him to a nearby rock. 'Sit there,' he ordered.

Zeke took an army canteen from his saddle. 'I'll get you some water.'

The scout walked along the shallow

167

edge of the soak until he could find a spot deep enough to fill the canteen. When it was full, he brought it back and held it up for Barney to drink. 'Get plenty of this into you. There's still a long ride ahead.'

The wounded man had a long drink and then said, 'That'll do for a while. Just put the stopper back. I'll have more later.'

After asking Jim to secure the horses, Zeke took up his rifle and slipped away into the trees. In seconds he had disappeared from view. The two cowboys settled down in the shade to wait.

Barney left his rock and sat down in the soft grass at the base of a tree but Jim was restless. He wondered if Zeke was really concerned about the soak being a possible trap — the scout had carelessly showed himself at the water's edge. He half expected Zeke to have a very cursory look around and then return fairly quickly to announce that all was clear, but the time dragged on and by the position of the sun above the trees, he estimated that at least half an hour had passed. Zeke was either being very cautious or had run into trouble. The marshy area was about two hundred yards across and approximately a quarter of a mile long. It was possible that the scout was working slowly through the tree line on its perimeter but Jim felt a growing sense of unease.

'Zeke's been gone a long time,' Barney complained. 'We'll be all hours gettin' back to town tonight. This arm is givin' me hell, I wish he'd hurry.'

Jim moved a little closer to the edge of the trees. 'I'll have a look across the swamp and see if I can sight him. If all's clear he might signal from over there for us to bring the horses around.'

Keeping under cover the cowboy moved along the edge of the swamp and strained his eyes to see any movement on the other side. He saw nothing moving. But then his eye fell on the water's edge on his side of the swamp. The footprints in the mud struck him as being unusual and he looked around for more. Then he was sure.

Hurrying back to Barney he said, 'We have to move from here real quick.'

'Why?' the wounded man demanded. He was comfortable where he was.

'Because Crooked Foot's here.'

16

'What are you talkin' about? Ain't he supposed to be dead?'

'He's not dead,' Jim said urgently. 'Zeke's Crooked Foot'

Barney was unconvinced. 'You're loco. He ain't got a crooked foot.'

'His foot's straight enough but when he puts down the right one, he turns it out more than normal. I can see it by the tracks he left in the mud. He leaves a strange track. Remember him saying back in White Rock that he had a broken foot once? You can bet he got the name from the other scouts or Indian trackers after they saw his trail.'

Barney was thoroughly alarmed and struggled to his feet by grasping the tree trunk with his good hand. 'Then he's probably in cahoots with that pair of prospectors that we let go. It was their ponies made those tracks we found. He sent them here ahead of us. That mangy sonofabitch has lured us into a trap.'

'I reckon so. He knows where we are and he knows you're wounded. I think they'll be sneaking up on us right now.' As he spoke Jim collected both their rifles from where they hung on the horses. He paused and checked the way the trees were moving. 'Zeke's not dumb enough to come straight across the swamp. The wind's blowing from the west. They won't come that way because the horses might smell them and give the game away. They'll come in from over there on the east.'

'I take it we ain't runnin'.'

'You're right, Barney. Chances are that they'd catch up with us somewhere else. It might be better to surprise them here. Let's just move back away from the horses to a place that will allow us to cover where Zeke left us. If we're lucky they'll come creeping in between us and the soak and we'll get a good view of them.'

'Ain't you forgettin' that I can't use a

rifle and if I empty my Colt shootin' left-handed, I won't be able to reload. It could be you against all three of them.'

Jim passed his revolver to Barney. 'I'll have both rifles. This will give you an extra six shots. I need you in a position to cover my back. Now, let's get moving.'

The two moved deeper into the trees and Jim found a spot where a tree had fallen leaving a hole partially concealed by a tangle of exposed roots and tall weeds. 'Get down in there,' he told Barney. 'I'm going to get in among those little rocks and bushes. Leave the main shooting to me and only shoot if someone gets behind me. With any luck I might get one of them down before they realize that we're not where Zeke left us.'

Though neither said it, the fear that they had miscalculated was there. For all they knew the others might have already been watching them. With all senses alert the pair could only hope they had not been seen. Not without many misgivings they went to the selected positions and settled down to wait.

With a slight wind blowing through it, no forest is completely silent. Leaves brush against branches, twigs snap, birds and animals scuttle about in the foliage. When men are in fear of their lives they note sounds that under normal circumstances would be ignored. Everything depended upon seeing the attackers before they themselves were discovered.

Jim lay prone in the low bushes, his rifle thrust out before him so that he would not betray his position when he suddenly lifted it. Aware that movement is easily seen, he held as still as possible swivelling his eyes from side to side rather than turning his head. He found he was lying on a rock but forced himself to remain motionless. Then there came an urge to scratch his nose. He dared not think of sneezing or coughing in case his body reacted in accordance with his fears.

It was almost a relief when he heard

stealthy sounds in the brush. Someone was moving in on his left. He hoped that Barney had heard the sound but could not check to see. What if his friend had fallen asleep or lost consciousness because of his wound?

Then he saw the first sign of movement. A brown hat showed briefly above a bush about fifty yards away. Zeke's battered hat was dark grey so he was not the stranger. Where were the other two?

Fitch only had eyes for the horses as he inched his way through the undergrowth. Zeke had told him that the two cowboys would be nearby. Step by careful step, he crept forward, his rifle held ready for instant action. Idaho and Zeke were not far behind him, travelling parallel but keeping a few yards apart so that all had a clear line of fire. Though neither knew it, Zeke's approach was taking him behind Jim's position.

Barney could not see Fitch and Idaho but was shocked to see the scout moving stealthily behind where his partner was concealed. Forced to shoot left-handed, he was not sure that he would win a gun duel against Zeke but somehow he would need to warn Jim.

Already the latter's attention was otherwise engaged. For such a big man, Idaho was a quiet mover and when he suddenly came out of the brush, he was only a couple of yards from Jim. In two more steps he would be able to see over the bushes and discover the cowboy lying in wait.

Almost without thinking, Jim rolled on his side and fired his rifle at Idaho. He knew that he had not missed because his target was thrown backwards under the bullet's impact. Gambling that the man was out of the fight, he switched his aim to Fitch but the little man had seen what happened. He fired one hasty, inaccurate shot at Jim and went to ground.

Zeke knew by the shots that the two cowboys were close by and assumed that they were both still together. Aware that Fitch was creating a good distraction, he rose to his full height. He could see over low rocks and shrubs that sheltered Jim. A cloud of powder smoke was gathering over the position as the cowboy and Fitch exchanged shots.

With the gunfire masking any noise he was making, Zeke edged forward. He raised the rifle to his shoulder. At such close range he probably could have fired from the hip and hit his target but Zeke was not one to take chances. He had always relied upon good planning rather than luck.

Barney watched in horror as he saw Zeke about to shoot Jim and knew that he had to score a hit with his awkward left hand. He could not afford to wound his man and find himself involved in a gun duel. He cocked the Colt, rested his elbow on the edge of the hole and took aim. Every instinct told him to hurry but he knew that he had only one chance of doing the job properly. With his sights covering the centre of Zeke's buckskin jacket at the back, he squeezed the trigger.

Even as the hammer fell, Barney saw

his target moving slightly. The bullet that should have killed the scout, burned across his shoulder instead.

Self-preservation took over then and Zeke dived for cover before attempting to return the fire. He found a shallow ditch with a muddy bottom but the latter caused him no concern. He knew that he was somewhere dangerously close to two men who were as yet unseen. When he tried to see over the edge of the ditch, another shot from Barney kicked dirt in his face.

'Jim . . . Zeke's to your left . . . about twenty yards away.' The wounded man could do little more than shout a warning. It would only be a fluke if he hit a moving target shooting left-handed.

Jim snapped another couple of shots at Fitch before looking to his left. He detected movement in the shallow ditch that sheltered the scout and switched targets to send a couple of shots skimming just above the top of the bank.

Involuntarily the scout ducked as dirt and gravel sprayed around his face.

Barney took the chance of his life. While Zeke's head was down, he jumped to his feet and staggered across the intervening ground. He had to get close enough not to miss and could only hope that Fitch was fully occupied with Jim. Two steps from the ditch he halted and raised his revolver.

The scout had been taken completely by surprise. To his alarm, the cowhand was suddenly looming above him and sighting down the barrel of his Colt. But he was panting and shaky and the weapon looked awkward in the unfamiliar left hand. Trusting to luck, Zeke rolled sideways as he brought up his carbine. It was then that his luck ran out.

Barney's bullet ploughed down through the scout's shoulder and rolled him backwards. The rifle fell from his hands but with lightning reflexes, he clawed at his holstered revolver. It was barely clear of the leather when Barney fired another shot into him and continued firing until the hammer fell on a fired shell. Wasting no time, he dropped the gun and drew Jim's Colt from his belt. But he did not need it. Through a drifting haze of powder smoke, he saw Zeke staring skywards with sightless eyes.

'I got him, Jim.' There was no mistaking the triumphant note in his voice. 'I killed that murderin' sonofabitch.'

'Get under cover, there's still another one here.'

But the other one had no intention of remaining in the vicinity. Fitch knew that his luck had run out and tried to flee while his comrade was still attracting all the attention. He started sprinting from one tree to the next, but one tree was not wide enough to shelter him properly; he ran into a Winchester slug a split second before he started his dash for better cover.

Jim fired again at the fallen man. He did not see where Fitch's rifle was and could not afford to take chances.

'Stop shootin'.' Barney called. 'I can see him from here. He's a goner. We got the whole danged lot — got every one of them murderin' sonsabitches.'

17

'Wait where you are until I check on these three. Then I'll get you on your horse and we'll head for White Rock to get that arm fixed.'

Barney snorted in mock anger. 'I don't know what's keepin' your ears apart but it sure ain't brains. What was all this killin' about?'

'They were hiding a gold strike. Don't tell me that you want to go prospecting.'

'We don't have to. I reckon if we search these dead fellas we'll find a lot of gold. They were minin' that creek for weeks. What do you reckon Zeke was takin' off them dead ones before he gave the rest of their gatherin's to the Sioux? There's four families back in Texas waitin' for us to get their money back. Here's a chance of at least returnin' a bit of what they lost. I reckon I can walk enough to search these bodies. You go and find where those others left their horses and bring them back to here. Who knows what might be in a saddle-bag or rolled in a coat.'

'Will you be OK here for a while?'

'Of course I will. Now the sooner you get those horses, the sooner we can get movin'. The ride to White Rock is not gonna be a lot of fun.'

Jim wasted no time and found the horses easily. They had been tethered in the trees a couple of hundred yards away from where the fight had taken place. He led them back and secured them with the others.

Barney was not as well as he had pretended to be and was seated on a rock looking pale and haggard when his partner returned. But he managed a strained smile and pointed to the ground at his feet. There were three small buckskin bags and one slightly larger one, also a bundle of paper money. 'There's nuggets in them little bags and gold dust in the bigger one. Zeke was carryin' a lot of paper money too. He could have more in the saddle-bags on his horse but with one arm out of action, I thought I'd wait for you. That pony of Zeke's don't like strangers so watch it don't cow kick you.'

The animal laid back its ears and gave Jim an equine version of a scowl as he took the reins and stood close to the shoulder while removing the saddle-bags. It had been broken by Indians and was suspicious of white men.

They found more gold in Zeke's saddle-bags.

Jim shook his head in wonder. 'There's a fortune here, Barney. I reckon it should cover the twenty-four thousand dollars that Mason stole and there'll still be some left over. We can split that fifty-fifty. We know the gold's not stolen, although a lot of men died because of it. This really is our lucky day.'

Barney looked at his injured arm and croaked, 'Speak for yourself.'

Jim packed the gold into Zeke's saddle-bags and fastened them behind his own saddle. Then he collected the weapons and ammunition of the dead men — these could not be left to arm hostile tribesmen. Quickly he packed these onto the best of the ponies, a grey that Fitch had ridden. Then he removed the saddles and bridles from the two others and turned them loose.

Having neither the time nor the tools to bury the dead men, he left them to the scavengers.

Barney was getting weaker and it was difficult to get him aboard his tall horse but eventually he made it to the saddle. 'I'll be right now. Let's head for town. I hope you know the way.'

'I'll find the way. Just don't fall off that big elephant. From that height you could kill yourself.'

Jim mounted and took the reins of the pack animal. 'If we swing to our left, we should pick up the trail to White Rock.'

'Knowin' our luck, there'll be a great, big canyon between here and the trail,'

Barney mumbled. He was trying not to think of the long, pain-filled ride ahead.

Fortunately, the canyon that Barney had predicted, did not exist. The country was rough with uneven ground and patches of heavy brush. Progress was slow but they found no serious barriers and for the next couple of hours they plodded along in a south-easterly direction. There was little conversation and Barney rode slumped in his saddle. Jim was worried that his partner might lose consciousness and fall but the practice of long years on horseback and a grip on the horn kept him in place.

The sun was getting low when to the riders' intense relief, they came down a steep slope and suddenly found themselves on the White Rock trail.

★ ★ ★

The Brophys had been asleep for a couple of hours when Cassius started to bark.

'That's his warning bark,' Angela told her husband. 'Something's wrong.'

Nelson had reached the same conclusion. He rose quickly, struggled into the dressing gown and boots that he kept nearby, and picked up a loaded shotgun. 'Stay here and don't show any lights.'

He was about to leave the tent when they heard horses and a faint voice groaned, 'Shut your face, you noisy flea farm.'

'It's Barney,' Angela said as she too reached for her dressing gown and slippers.

As the doctor emerged he saw Jim already dismounted, supporting Barney in his saddle.

'Barney's been shot in the arm, Doc. He's all in. It's been a long ride.'

Angela arrived with a lantern in time to see the two men ease the wounded man from the horse and half carry him to the wagon. Henry Rhodes was now living at Buffalo's so the stretcher was vacant.

'Leave him to us now,' the doctor ordered as he cut away the blood-stained sleeve and improvised bandage.

The injured man groaned as Brophy examined the wound and cleaned it with surgical spirit. 'There's no bullet in it but the bone's broken,' he told his wife. 'Take the light well away and then bring me the ether.'

Jim was amazed. 'Are you going to set his broken arm in the dark?'

The doctor laughed. 'Of course not. But ether is very explosive and dangerous around any sort of flame. The ether will knock him out so that I can attend to that wound without causing him too much pain. When I put him to sleep, we can take the ether right away and bring back the lantern so I can see to set and repair that arm. Now leave him to us and get some rest yourself. You look nearly as bad as your friend.'

'I'll just fix the horses,' Jim said wearily, 'then I'll come back.' As an afterthought he said, 'I'll leave this pack here. I'm not up to putting things away at present.' But the truth of the matter was that he knew of nowhere safer to leave the precious saddle-bags. He was not really worried about the firearms they had collected.

He led the three horses to Dawson's corrals and allowed them a long drink at the water trough. Then he rubbed their backs and left them together in a smaller corral with a good supply of hay. He would settle up with Dawson in the morning. Entering the shed that housed their pack, he took a blanket, a canvas pack cover for a groundsheet and returned to the Brophy camp.

Barney's arm had been bandaged and splinted. He was conscious and was violently ill from the ether.

Angela said quietly to Jim. 'As soon as he gets the ether out of his system, he'll probably go to sleep. You should get some too. You have done all you can. Nelson and I will take over now.'

'I'll just settle down under your wagon so I'll be close if you need me. I don't know what we would have done without you and the doc. We were mighty lucky you were here.'

'We would not have been if Zeke had not told us to stay put until the army cleared the trail.' She paused, then asked, 'Have you seen Zeke? He left town yesterday morning leading another horse — seemed to be in a hurry.'

'We met up with Zeke. It's a long story but he's dead.'

'Oh no . . . That's awful — what happened?'

'Zeke and a couple of his white renegade friends have been behind the killings up at Antler Creek. At times I think he had the help of a few hostile Indians too. He had friends in both camps. They ambushed the Rowley party and had a good try at killing Barney and me. This time our luck was in and theirs ran out.'

'But why would he do that?' A note of disbelief was strong in Angela's tone. 'Zeke struck me as a man with high principles. He would not want to set the army and the Indians at each others' throats. You said it yourself, he had friends on both sides. What would he have to gain?'

'Zeke and his crew were covering up a gold strike. They killed anyone who got close and in the current climate, the Sioux got the blame. Zeke might have cared about the Indians once but gold does funny things to people.'

Jim could see that Angela was not fully convinced. 'Have you heard the name Crooked Foot?'

'Of course I have. That was a nickname of Zeke's from his scouting days. A few of his old friends called him that. There was nothing secret about that name.'

'It wasn't a secret to those who knew him but he sure didn't want us to find out about it. Zeke knew that Barney and I were strangers who had heard a dying renegade name Crooked Foot was their leader. When I asked about the name he carried on as though it was a great secret about a mysterious Sioux war chief. He told us two dumb cowhands not to mention the name because of the effect it might have on restless Lakota who were looking for a leader. We kept the secret but now I know why those night attacks were made here: Zeke was trying to silence us before we let slip what we knew. We killed an Indian that day we rescued those prospectors. Zeke told us it was Crooked Foot but Barney knew something was wrong when he saw your sketch of a Crow scout. The redskin we killed had that same hairstyle: he was a Crow working for Zeke. Yesterday Zeke was leading us into an ambush when I saw the crooked track he left in the mud and we woke up just in time. They had a good try at killing us but we were lucky.'

'It's still hard to imagine Zeke as a cold-blooded killer.'

'Gold changes people. Zeke and his friends were picking up easily found gold along Antler Creek. They knew that Andrews, the surveyor, was sure to find what they were up to and a gold rush would start. That's why the party was almost wiped out. They let Henry Rhodes escape to keep people scared to go into the area. The discovery couldn't be hidden forever but Crooked Foot and his friends resorted to murder for the sake of collecting as much gold as they could before the rush started.'

'Is there much gold there?'

'There's some but it would take a proper miner to work out just how much.' Choosing his words carefully, Jim said in a low voice, 'Barney and I found enough on some of those renegades to prove that there is gold along the creek. We're sort of keeping it as our reward for making the new mining site safer.'

Angela asked no more probing questions. Her experience in the west had taught her that private business was just that. If information was not volunteered, it was bad manners to ask. Instead she told Jim, 'You look worn out. Why don't you rest now. Nelson and I will make sure that Barney is settled down and then go back to bed. Call us if you think he might be in trouble.'

'He'll be in trouble if he wakes me.' Angela hoped he was only joking.

18

The day that followed was a busy one. Jim, as was his habit, rose early but tried to be as quiet as possible for he knew that the Brophys had enjoyed even less sleep than he had. Peering under the canvas hood of the wagon, he saw that Barney appeared to be sleeping peacefully.

Cassius roused himself from where he was stretched in the morning sun and strolled over to Jim. He wagged his tail as the cowboy stroked his head. 'How are you today, Cassius?'

Angela was just emerging from the tent and overheard him. She laughed. 'I think you would get quite a shock if he answered.'

'Maybe I would but sometimes I think they understand us more than we understand them. I know it sounds crazy but I talk to most animals I work with. Folks say it's a waste of time because they don't speak English but I'm not sure they're right.'

'At least you talk to him more politely than Barney does.'

Barney's voice came from the inside of the wagon. 'Are you two discussing me?'

'So you're back with us,' Jim said in a tone of exaggerated disappointment. 'Some folks will do anything for a bit of extra time in bed.'

'Glad to see that you didn't get too upset about me nearly gettin' killed. What's the doc say about me gettin' up?'

Angela replied, 'I'll check with him and let you know. Meanwhile you stay put. I have told Cassius to attack you if you try to get up before I'm back.'

Jim climbed into the wagon. 'How's the arm feel?'

'It's sore but at least I still have it. What's been happenin'?'

'Nothing yet but we still have to tell a few people about Zeke. Someone might

196

want to collect what's left of Rowley's party and plant them properly too.'

'What do we tell folks about the gold?'

'I guess that all we can do is say that Zeke reckoned there was gold on Antler Creek and didn't want anyone else near it.'

'Folks are gonna ask how we knew about the gold.'

Jim shrugged his shoulders. 'We'll just say that Zeke had some gold on him but we're keeping it to cover expenses. No one need know how much.'

A doubtful expression crossed Barney's face. 'There's some won't like that.'

'Too bad — but I doubt that anyone will wait around for long. I reckon there'll be a rush to Antler Creek.'

'Do you think we should join the rush?'

'You can if you like but I'm heading for home. There's some folks who'll be mighty pleased to see at least some of their money back and if there's any left over we might be able to get our own ranch. I'm no miner. I don't like scratching around in the dirt.'

'Me either,' Barney agreed. 'If a job can't be done on horseback, it ain't worth doin'.'

'There's one more job here that I'm not exactly keen on. Someone has to break the news about Zeke and the gold. He had a few friends here if I recall. I reckon a few of those might not be happy that we stopped his clock.'

'That's too bad. None of them thought to do it. Zeke's lies have kept folks in town for weeks scared to travel and expectin' an injun attack.'

'I might take those rifles and six-shooters we collected over to Murphy and see if he can sell them for us. Dawson told me that he does a bit of second-hand dealing. We might be able to make a few bucks out of them.'

Barney used his good hand to scratch his head. 'They won't bring much. Why not just give them away?'

Jim explained, 'We need to make folks think that we didn't make much out of killing Zeke and his compadres. You can bet there are enough hard cases around here who would slit our throats for one tenth of what we have. If they see us being careful with our money, they won't be so suspicious. But if you agree we could give away a couple of things.'

'Such as?'

'That grey pony we brought in is nice and gentle. I figured we'd give it to Mrs Brophy. We'll pay the doc in cash but folks will think that the horse is payment for fixing your arm.'

'That makes sense. What else?'

'We could give one of those 'sixty-six Winchesters to Henry Rhodes along with some cartridges. Since Zeke won't be around Buffalo doesn't have a hunter. Henry might be able to make a bit shooting game for him. The kid doesn't have much but the rifle might help him get started again.'

'I won't argue with that but if he goes

bad and starts robbin' banks and coaches I'll tell everyone it was your idea. And while you're makin' so free with our cash what about gettin' me a new shirt from the general store? You might remember rippin' up my old one.'

'Think yourself lucky you still need a shirt. But I can see the doc coming so I'll get moving.'

★　★　★

When Jim told his news, he and Barney soon became the town's most sought-after inhabitants. They would have left White Rock except that the doctor wished to ensure that the wound to Barney's arm was healing properly before he put on a more permanent plaster cast. Gold fever had gripped the town and several times in the days that followed, strangers would seek out the pair and question them at length about Antler Creek. Zeke and the real possibility of Indian attacks was forgotten. Men were organizing groups and buying supplies and a couple of more enterprising types had ridden out for the new goldfield within hours of Jim's announcement.

It was while delivering the rifle and ammunition to Henry that the pair learned some disturbing news. After profuse thanks the boy said, 'I was coming to see you fellows today. I overheard a couple of rough-looking characters at breakfast planning to rob you. They didn't know I was on the other side of a very thin wall. They reckoned that you had already collected a heap of gold otherwise you would be staking claims at Antler Creek. One of them said that taking gold was a lot easier than digging for it.'

'Sounds like they're speaking from experience,' Jim said. 'Do you know who they are?'

The boy shook his head. 'I've seen them around a couple of times and I'm pretty sure they were with Zeke but I don't know their names. They're both big men, maybe thirty or so. One has a bushy light brown beard and the other has long, straggly black hair. The one with the brown beard was wearing one of those floppy black hats like soldiers wear. Both of them were wearing two guns and look like they've had plenty of practice with them. Be careful.'

Barney frowned and looked at Jim. 'How do we handle this? I'm not much use in a gunfight at present.'

His partner thought for a while. Then he said, 'I'm going to make a run for Belle Fourche. Dawson told me they have a bank there that will buy the gold and convert it to cash. I can have cheques posted to the four families who are waiting for us to catch Mason. Those gunmen won't trouble anyone around here if they know that I have the gold and I intend letting them know that I'm carrying it.'

'You're crazy. What if they catch up with you? There's injuns out there too.'

'Not too many horses can catch that one of mine.'

'A bullet will,' Barney reminded him.

'I could go with you,' Henry said eagerly. He was anxious to try out his new armaments.

'No,' Jim said. 'It's best that you stay here. If I can't manage to lure those characters away, they might have a try at Barney or even the doc and his wife. An extra gun might be needed more here than out on the trail.'

Both Jim and Barney knew that for all his eagerness, Henry might not have been much use in a gunfight and neither wanted to involve innocent third parties in their own troubles. With sincere thanks and the assurance that he would be called upon if needed, the boy went back to his work.

Barney disliked the idea of Jim taking all the risk but knew that he himself would be more of a hindrance than a help.

His partner returned to Dawson's to attend to their animals and later took a new shirt down to Barney. The latter was preparing to leave when Doc Brophy joined them.

'You really should stay around here,' the doctor told the wounded cowboy, 'so that I can keep a check on that arm.'

'It might be better if I go up to our camp at Dawson's. There could be gunplay around me and Jim, and we don't want to get you people into our fight.'

Angela had just arrived on the scene with a sketch pad under her arm and Cassius at her heels. 'What's this about a fight?'

The two cowhands explained.

'You stay right here,' Angela said sternly. 'You are still our patient. Quite possibly those gunmen will try to follow Jim but if they don't and come around here I'll set Cassius onto them.'

Barney was tempted to mention the fact that dogs were not bullet-proof but decided to save his breath. Angela was wearing a very determined look and so was her husband.

'Look down the street,' Doc Brophy said. 'Those two men with horses fit the description of the gunmen Henry was talking about. They have their horses saddled and might be leaving town.'

Jim disagreed. 'They are loosening their cinches and keeping their horses handy on the hitching rail in case they need them in a hurry.'

'Do you think they'll try anything in town?' Angela said nervously.

'Too many people about,' Barney grunted. 'They'll wait for a quieter time.'

'They won't get one,' Jim snapped. 'My horse is fit and ready to go. I'll get him and make my run in daylight. That should draw them away from here.'

Barney was worried. 'You don't want them catchin' you alone out there in the hills.'

'I'll go cross-country so they won't really know where I'm headed and after dark I'll change direction when they can't track me. I've never been to Belle Fourche but I know its general direction. By morning I should be close enough to settled places to ask directions.'

The others were still doubtful of the plan's success when Jim came back leading his saddled horse.

'Where's your Winchester?' Barney demanded.

'It's with our pack at Dawson's. I'll be running not fighting.'

'You can't go out without a coat,' the doctor protested. 'The nights are still very cold.'

'I'd sooner catch a cold than catch lead poisoning, Doc. A long, fast ride like this is all about weight. The less the horse has to carry, the better. As it is, there'll be extra weight in the saddle-bags. Where are they?'

Angela pointed under the wagon. 'Cassius is guarding them.'

Jim was about to pick up the bags but the dog curled its lip and gave a warning growl.

'When we tell him to watch something he really watches it,' Angela laughed as she took the bags and passed them to Jim.

Hidden behind the wagon, he fastened the saddle-bags and mounted. 'I'll see you in a couple of days,' he said as he turned his horse out into the street.

Hoping not to attract too much attention from the general public, he allowed the horse to walk briskly. Had he looked behind, Jim would have seen the man with the floppy, black hat run into Murphy's saloon to alert his long-haired friend.

Long Hair was reluctant to leave the saloon. 'There's no hurry. We can't do anything to him too close to town and there's plenty of light to track him.'

His companion was not convinced. 'That *hombre* outsmarted our old friend Crooked Foot and he was no fool. I reckon he's carrying Crooked Foot's gold. The sneaky sonofabitch always hinted he had found gold but killed a lot of people to keep its whereabouts a secret. Now put down that drink. We have some riding to do.'

★   ★   ★

Jim was heading north-east across a wide expanse of rolling prairie when he saw that he was being followed. Looking along his back trail he saw two tiny dots descending a low butte. He would not have worried if he had not travelled the same route a short while earlier. The newcomers were following his tracks.

A lift of the rein and a very light touch of the spurs sent the brown horse into a canter. The increased pace would raise dust and if the men behind had not sighted him yet, the dust would attract their attention. With a long start and a good horse, Jim could expect to stay out of accurate rifle range but if the horse stepped in a hole or went lame for some reason the situation suddenly could change. He had to get clear of the open country too in case it became necessary to turn on his pursuers. Otherwise the hunters could stay out of revolver range and pick him off with their rifles.

An hour passed and the two riders were still behind and looked to have gained on their quarry. Jim was holding down the pace, sometimes trotting, cantering where the ground underfoot was safe enough and maintaining a fast walk through difficult areas. He changed course slightly just in case the others just happened to be travelling in the same general direction but they stayed on his trail. Each time he looked, he could see that they had gained ground but the hunters had no idea of the distance that lay ahead. They were content to push a little harder to close the gap even though doing so took more out of their horses.

Jim had been weighing up the advantages of certain spots to ambush his hunters but several miles passed before he found one that really suited his purposes.

When he reached a line of low bluffs rising from the plain he sought a place to turn on his pursuers. The two riders had abandoned all stealth and increased their speed. They knew that they were safe from the presence of witnesses.

The brown horse jumped into a

gallop at the light touch of the spurs and raced straight at the line of light green cottonwoods along the base of the bluff. The rider's initial idea had been to change direction again and then escape while screened by the trees but he found himself on a game trail leading to the small creek at the foot of the bluffs. He halted briefly to allow his horse a few mouthfuls of water and saw across the stream a narrow path coming down from the heights. This offered a way out of his problem if his luck held. It would be steep but he had ridden the same horse in worse places. The creek was only fetlock deep as he rode through it and set his mount up the narrow path that wild animals had used to gain access to the water. It followed the uneven contours of the bluff as it wound its way up the steep clay walls. Jim noted with satisfaction that the path could be ascended or descended but turning around was out of the question. When he reached level ground, the two riders were just disappearing into the cottonwoods below. They were not far behind their quarry.

There was just time to ride the horse to a place where it could not be seen from the path, leave it ground-tied and hurry back. Then he crawled to the edge of the bank overlooking the trail, drew his Colt and waited.

'We're gaining on him,' a voice announced as the horses splashed across the creek. 'The trail's still wet with water that dripped off his horse.' There followed a grunting of horses, a creaking of leather and the sound of hoofs cutting into the hard clay.

The sounds came closer and suddenly a hat appeared below where Jim lay waiting.

It would have been a simple thing to shoot the man but Jim had never liked killing. Instead, he lashed out with the barrel of his gun, hit Long Hair in the forehead and knocked him from the saddle. The man fell over the edge of the narrow track and rolled thirty feet to the bottom of the slope. His black-hatted companion shouted in surprise as he found himself looking into the barrel of a Colt .45 from a distance of a couple of paces; he could not retreat and to go ahead was suicide. Ashen-faced, the man raised his hands.

'Join him,' the prey-turned-hunter ordered and gestured with his gun toward the point where Long Hair had disappeared.

For one so surprised the man obeyed very quickly. He jumped from his saddle, tried to keep upright, failed, and in a shower of dust and loose gravel slid and tumbled back down the slope. The horses could not turn around and when Jim fired a shot in the air, they plunged forward up the narrow path. He caught them as they reached the level ground, led both to where his own horse waited and mounted. Both men's rifles were still on the saddles so he had little to fear from long-range shooting even if the two were fit enough to climb the bluff and fire on him. After covering a couple of miles and seeing the sun rapidly setting, he halted, unsaddled both captured animals and turned them loose at a spot of good grazing. He took both bridles with him, waiting until dark to throw them away. In the unlikely event that his hunters somehow recovered their mounts there was little chance that they could pursue him.

He was ravenously hungry and the temperature was dropping as darkness fell. Aware of the uncomfortable night ahead Jim was tempted to keep moving but he had to keep his mount in good condition. He allowed it a drink at a small waterhole and then rode on until he found a patch of good grazing. There he unsaddled, rubbed his horse's back and found a patch of bare, dusty ground where it could roll. The tired animal grunted with pleasure as it rolled, then rose and shook off the dust. When it was grazing at the end of his lariat, its owner stretched out to get some rest himself.

A couple of hours of sheer misery

followed and he sat wrapped in a sweaty saddle blanket and tried to doze. The night had turned cold and Jim began to wonder at the wisdom of leaving his coat behind. The temptation to build a fire was strong but stray bands of Indians were known to hunt in the area and it could attract them. From considerable distances they could smell smoke from the most carefully concealed fires.

Half an hour before sunrise Jim was riding northeast again. He hit a stream flowing in the direction he needed to go so followed it. After about a mile he came across a half-breed trapper's cabin. The owner confirmed that the river was the Belle Fourche and that if all went well, he would reach the town by mid-afternoon. It was about that time when he halted his weary horse in front of the bank and entered it carrying his saddle-bags.

The teller, a young man with thin features and dark hair looked up nervously. The saddle-bags on Jim's shoulder made him suspect that the latter might have been thinking of an unauthorized withdrawal. He looked relieved when the newcomer announced, 'I have some gold here that I want to turn into cash.'

'Just wait a second, sir. I'll get our manager, Mr Murdoch, he handles our gold buying.'

When Jim emerged later he had arranged for four cheques, each of six thousand dollars, to be sent to the four ranches who had sent the cattle north. The balance, approximately eighteen hundred dollars, he took in cash to split with Barney.

Their job was over, it was time to go home.

19

When Jim reached White Rock three days later, he was greeted with great relief but then Barney had news that stopped him in his tracks.

'Our job ain't over yet. Mason's still alive. He's hidin' out in the army.'

'How do you know?'

'Because Angela Brophy painted his picture in Bismarck a couple of weeks ago. I've seen it. It's the spittin' image of that little coyote. She said he posed for drinkin' money but the likeness is too good to be someone else. He's at Fort Lincoln in North Dakota. We have to get there before he deserts or gets shifted someplace else.'

'What about your arm?'

Barney displayed a new plaster cast on the arm he had in a sling. 'The outside bullet damage has healed so the doc was able to replace the bandages and splint with a proper cast. Of course you'll have to help me saddle my horse and do a few other things, but at least I'm fit to ride again.'

Later the pair visited the Brophys, as they were packing their wagon to leave. The Indian threat was over and half the town had already departed for the new goldfield on Antler Creek.

Angela stopped packing long enough to display the painting. There was no mistaking Mason; she had even captured his shifty look.

'There's hundreds of men in a cavalry regiment,' Jim said. 'How will we find him?'

Angela pointed to the soldier's cap. 'That number above the badge is the regiment and the letter under the badge is the man's troop. With that number and the right letter you will only have to pick him from fifty or sixty men.'

'We've got him,' Barney said with great glee. 'We will finally nail that little — ' He remembered that Angela was nearby and ceased to describe

Mason in the colourful terms he had intended.

'How's that grey pony going'?' Jim asked Angela.

'He's lovely but I think Cassius is jealous.'

'Don't take any notice of that sonofabitch,' Barney said solemnly.

For a second Angela looked shocked and angry, then she saw that Barney was trying to keep a straight face. 'I suppose you're right, Barney, but if I thought you were trying to insult my dog, I'd break your other arm.'

'I wouldn't do that but you have to admit the facts. The four-legged ones are all right. It's the two-legged ones that give you trouble.'

'Where are you going now?' Jim asked.

Doc Brophy replied. 'We might head for the new gold field at Antler Creek. There'll be folks needing our services there by now. After a few days the shootings and accidents start happening. There's sure to be someone needing a doctor.'

'They sure will,' Barney told them. 'Buffalo is headin' there and young Henry is goin' with him. You might need to start workin' on an antidote for that coffee of his.'

'We'll miss you folks. You've been extra good to Barney and me. If you ever come to the San Matteo Valley in Texas, just ask for us. Folks around there will know where we are.'

'And bring your flea farm,' Barney said with a sly grin.

Angela laughed and swatted him with her hat.

An hour later, the two cowhands were at Dawson's corrals when they saw the Brophys leave. Nelson was driving the wagon while Angela rode beside on her grey pony. Cassius trotted at its heels.

Barney saw her looking their way and waved. 'Real nice folks,' he told Jim. 'Even old Cassius wasn't too bad. Angela sure thought the world of that lanky old hound. Are all English ladies crazy about dogs, or is it just her?'

'How the hell would I know? I've never met an English lady before.'

'When do you reckon we should be lookin' up Mister Mason?'

'Let's give my horse a day's rest and then we'll make our way up the Missouri to Fort Lincoln. This time we really do know where to find that thieving rat.'

* * *

A week later the partners halted their horses on the outskirts of Fort Abraham Lincoln in North Dakota. They had reached Bismark on the river's west bank the previous day, stayed there overnight and crossed to the fort the following morning.

It was not the small log-palisaded fortification that was common throughout the west but a collection of modern two-storey buildings, barracks and sheds on a large plain beside the river. The buildings surrounded a spacious parade ground that appeared to be a hive of activity. Onlookers in civilian clothes and military uniforms surrounded the perimeter and the partners heard band music while the sun glinted on highly polished instruments.

Barney chuckled. 'I can't wait to see the look on Mason's rat face when we turn up and have him arrested.'

'I'm not sure it will do us any good.' Jim was more worried. 'If he's in the army, it's because he somehow lost all that money. That's a hell of a lot to lose in a year. He sure couldn't drink it out.'

'A man with that much money can always count on friends who will help him to lose it. If half what we learned about him is true, Mason was a crazy gambler. I hope he tries to get away because I'll be mighty pleased to put a bullet in him.'

'Shooting left-handed?'

They rode closer.

'Now where would you boys be going?'

The questioner was a big man with

the red chevrons of an artillery sergeant on the sleeve of his dark blue coat. Four men in privates' uniforms accompanied him.

'We're after a thief who stole a whole heap of money,' Jim explained. 'He's hiding out in the cavalry. We want him arrested.'

The sergeant laughed and pointed to a group of anxious-looking civilians not far away. 'All them fellows there have similar stories. They're shopkeepers, saloon owners, gamblers and even the odd lawman but we don't allow them any closer. The cavalry are going out after the Sioux and nobody will be released from the ranks. When the campaign is over you can try again but it could be months before they come back.'

'We ain't got months,' Barney protested. 'We have to head back to Texas.'

The soldier shrugged. 'That's your problem. But anyone in those ranks at present stays in them until the campaign is over. It's General Terry's orders. He's the big boss here but there's a few other famous soldiers going out as well. Now if you behave yourselves you can wait and see the show. I'm warning you though, don't cause any trouble.'

'We're flogging a dead horse here,' Jim told Barney. 'All things considered it has turned out pretty good for us. Let's forget Mason and start for home.'

'You're right. We may as well quit while we're ahead. But first I'm curious to see if that little rat's still in the army. For all we know he might have deserted.' He asked the sergeant, 'Is there anywhere we can get close enough to see the soldiers?'

The soldier pointed. 'There's a road over there about a hundred yards away. The cavalry regiment will march out that way as they leave the fort. By then the big show will be over. You boys will get a good view from up there on your horses. You can see all the senior officers assembling over there near those flags. That's the saluting base.

223

There's a whole heap of generals and such here to see off the cavalry. The regiment will pass them in review in column of troops. They'll do one turn around the parade ground, form up in fours and then march off. The transport wagons and pack train will follow behind.'

The band broke into a lively tune. 'That's Garryowen,' the soldier explained. 'It's an old Irish drinking tune that's the regimental march. The colour party is coming into view now.'

A mounted group bearing several flags came onto the parade ground and a short distance behind, a cavalry troop in a broad, single rank wheeled into view. The inside riders barely moved while those at the outside end of the line moved at a smart trot to keep the line straight. Swinging like a gate on a hinge, the troop rounded the corner and marched forward.

They made a fine sight with uniforms clean, metal and leather polished, and horses groomed until their coats shone.

Jim watched the unfolding scene for a couple of seconds and then asked, 'How do we know which is C troop?'

'The troops will parade in alphabetical order. C troop should be the third one. Each troop has the same colour horses. The troop number is also shown on that red and white guidon.'

Jim stood in his stirrups and shaded his eyes against the morning sun. 'I can't see the letter on the flag but that third troop are all riding sorrels. Mason's probably with them — if he hasn't deserted already.'

The sergeant told them, 'That's Captain Tom's troop. They're a hard bunch. Don't start anything with them or you'll find yourself fighting the whole troop. Two no-goods from that outfit tried to murder Wild Bill Hickok in Hayes City. Bill killed one and wounded the other. They needed shooting too but the whole troop came after him and ran Wild Bill out of town. Don't think of upsetting that bunch.'

After the twelve troops had passed in

review, they formed into columns of fours and a colourful group of Indians and white scouts galloped out to the head of the parade. Behind them came a mounted group of officers and civilians.

'There's two women with that bunch,' Barney observed. 'Don't tell me they're goin' after the Sioux.'

'That's the general's wife and his sister. She's married to another of the officers. They're going with the column as far as the first camp. There's damn near enough of the general's relatives to take on the Sioux on their own. He has a couple of brothers: Tom is command-ing C troop; another is a civilian contractor of some kind and a nephew is also going with him. There's even a newspaper man. If there's one thing Iron Ass likes to control it's his own publicity. I can see the wagon train coming into view. You boys should go over to the side of the road now. A troop will be passing by soon so C won't be far behind. Now don't do anything rash if you see your man.'

'There ain't no justice in the world,' Barney complained as they rode closer to where the regiment was passing. 'Mason must have lost all that money or he wouldn't be a thirteen-dollar-a-month soldier. He should be made to pay for robbin' our folks.'

The sorrel horse troop came into view and the two cowboys scanned the passing faces.

Suddenly Jim said, 'There he is . . . in the third rank on this side.'

There was no mistaking the pinched features with a beaky nose and small, slitted eyes. The moustache was slightly larger but its wearer was Mason.

'You thievin' sonofabitch!' Barney roared. 'You won't get away with what you did.'

At first Mason looked startled but then realized that he was safe. He looked briefly, enough to identify the speaker and sneered contemptuously as he rode past.

Jim put a restraining hand on

Barney's shoulder. 'Let him go. We got the money our folks needed thanks to Crooked Foot. It's time we went home. Mason's luck won't last for ever.'

Barney took a last look as the Seventh Cavalry followed General Custer on what was to be his last campaign. 'You're right, Jim.' He lifted his reins and turned his horse away. 'We've been away from Texas too long. To hell with Mason. He's a sneaky little skunk and it's hard just to sit here and see him ride away. Maybe though, out there against the Sioux, he'll find himself in a situation where his tricks don't work.'

Jim turned his horse. 'Forget him, Barney. Time we were going home. We've been away too long.'

THE END

Other titles in the
Linford Western Library:

TRAIL OF THE HANGED MAN

Steve Hayes

Haunted by a missing past, Ben Lawless heads for Arizona to start a new life. On the way he provokes Joey Morgan's wrathful vengeance when he prevents him from hanging Sheriff Tishman. Then he helps his neighbour, Ingrid Bjorkman, to fight Stillman Stadtlander, a ruthless cattle baron who wants her land. Lawless will do anything for the beautiful Ingrid. But this deadly conflict will begin a series of perilous events that will lead him to the man who hanged him . . .

SHOTGUN MESSENGER

Colin Bainbridge

The outlaws' first mistake was to shoot Rhett Coulter's dog. He wasn't a man to mess with, Norman Roberts and his gang of gunslicks discovered. And when Coulter's friend's ranch, the Block H, is burned down, his woman barely escapes with her life — another reason to put Roberts out of business — quite apart from the little matter of his hoard of stolen bullion. Coulter fights overwhelming odds, while events rapidly draw him towards the final, blistering showdown . . .

SMOKING BARRELS

John Ladd

Steve Hardie arrives in Cripple Creek and becomes involved in a scuffle with a bunch of drunken cowpokes. Bravely, he saves the life of the local sheriff, but accidentally kills one of the cowboys. Nobody kills one of Hyram Slade's men and lives, so he rides out of town. Only Hardie's death will satisfy Slade and he quickly leads his hired henchmen in pursuit. And, in a close confrontation with Slade, death beckons Steve. Can he survive another day?

LONESOME RANGE

Tyler Hatch

He had many names. He was the fastest gun in Texas, Colorado, or just about anywhere. When he was recognized, the challengers would come, guns would blaze and he'd ride away from yet another dead man. Then came the day where he'd killed one too many and the fastest gun had to swap his Colt for a sledge on the rockpile — for ten long years. But a chance for freedom came along, and he grabbed it with both hands . . .

WYOMING DOUBLE-CROSS

J. D. Kincaid

The notorious Blair Wilton and his gang of outlaws plot to raid the bank at Medicine Bow, first sending Chicago confidence trickster Paul Springer to reconnoitre the town. But here, Springer encounters an old acquaintance and suddenly changes his plans. Meanwhile, the outlaws' woes increase when Jack Stone, the famous Kentuckian gunfighter, enters into the fray and goes up against Wilton and his gang. Will it be Stone or Wilton who survives the final, deadly confrontation?